*Samuel French Acting Edition*

# George A. Romero's Night of the Living Dead™ Live

*Written by* Christopher Bond, Dale Boyer & Trevor Martin

*Created by* Christopher Harrison & Phil Pattison

SAMUELFRENCH.COM    SAMUELFRENCH.CO.UK

### FOR PRODUCTION ENQUIRIES

UNITED STATES AND CANADA
Info@SamuelFrench.com
1-866-598-8449

UNITED KINGDOM AND EUROPE
Plays@SamuelFrench.co.uk
020-7255-4302

Each title is subject to availability from Samuel French, depending upon country of performance. Please be aware that *NIGHT OF THE LIVING DEAD™ LIVE* may not be licensed by Samuel French in your territory. Professional and amateur producers should contact the nearest Samuel French office or licensing partner to verify availability.

## MUSIC USE NOTE

## IMPORTANT BILLING AND CREDIT REQUIREMENTS

Based on the original film *Night of the Living Dead* written by George A. Romero & John Russo and produced by Russ Streiner

First produced by Nictophobia Films in Toronto in 2013

Recorded sound effects and music by
Jamie Lamb and Mike Trebilcock

"Work Together" written by
Christopher Bond, Jamie Lamb & Trevor Martin

Track arrangement by Jamie Lamb & Mike Trebilcock

*NIGHT OF THE LIVING DEAD*™ *LIVE* premiered at the Theatre Passe Muraille in Toronto, Ontario in April 2013 under the direction of Christopher Bond, with sets by Lindsay Anne Black, lighting by Michelle Ramsey, costumes by Claudia Kada, sound design by Richard Feren, special FX by Carlos Henriques, and makeup by Christina Spina. The cast was as follows:

**BEN / VARIOUS** ..................................... Darryl Hinds
**HARRY / VARIOUS**.......................... Mike "Nug" Nahrgang
**BARBRA / KAREN / VARIOUS** .................... Gwynne Phillips
**TOM / JOHNNY / VARIOUS** ..................... Andrew Fleming
**HELEN / JUDY / VARIOUS**........................... Dale Boyer
**CHIEF MCCLELLAND / WHITE BEN / VARIOUS** ...... Trevor Martin

# CHARACTERS

**BARBRA** – Early/mid-twenties, woman. Traditional and put-together at first, but as the events unfold, digresses into a child-like state.

**BEN** – African American man in his late twenties. A "leading man" type. Heroic. Outspoken. Protective of Barbra.

**TOM** – Young man. Handsome. Bright-eyed. Judy's boyfriend.

**JUDY** – Young woman. Tom's girlfriend. Girl next door.

**HARRY** – Late thirties. Curmudgeonly, working-class man. Weaselly and antagonistic. Helen's husband and Karen's father.

**HELEN** – Late thirties. Dry, world-weary homemaker. Unamused wife of Harry. Mother of Karen.

**CHIEF MCCLELLAND** – Late thirties, small-town sheriff. Folksy and pragmatic.

**VINCE** – Chief McClelland's young deputy. Local volunteer. A little idealistic. Obedient to the chief.

**KAREN** – Nine-year-old daughter of Harry and Helen.

# SETTING & TIME

Rural Pennsylvania. Late 1960s.

## AUTHOR'S NOTES

Bells and whistles are great, but they aren't necessary for the success of this production. Creativity wins, no matter the budget.

We had a cast of six, all playing multiple roles. Use as many performers as you want. Keep in mind, there are some Judy/Helen lines that have a double meaning, commenting on the ridiculous quick changes the actor had to do when double-cast in those roles. At face value, they still make sense.

We offer a terrific music package, composed by Mike Trebilcock, that beautifully highlights the action while paying tribute to the original film's score. If you choose not to use it, we suggest you find a creative way to cover the scene changes. Tracks for the finale song, "Work Together," are also available. We strongly encourage you to use them.

Special note on video: In Act I, scene 11, we used projected clips, cut from the film, to show the audience what Harry is seeing out the window. The times provided in the script are approximate depending on the copy of the film, but we describe the action Harry is watching. If you choose not to use the film clips, you can create a live representation of those scenes from the film.

It was an honor to be the official theatrical production of George A. Romero's horror masterpiece. We'd like to acknowledge him, along with Russ Streiner and John Russo, who were extremely generous with their time and thoughts on the project. Their support and guidance were critical to the success of the production.

*For George.*
*Thank you.*

# ACT I

### Scene One

*(Lights up, revealing the disheveled living room of an old farmhouse. The murmur of male voices and barking dogs are heard in the distance. The sound of a helicopter passes overhead.)*

*(**BEN** slowly enters from the basement door. He is holding a rifle. He cautiously looks outside the front window.)*

*(Bang! A gunshot hits **BEN** in the head. Blood splatters onto the wall behind him as he collapses.)*

*(Blackout.)*

**[MUSIC CUE NO. 01]**

## Scene Two

*(Lights up on* **CHIEF MCCLELLAND** *peering over the shoulder of* **VINCE**, *who is holding a smoking rifle.* **VINCE** *goes toward the house to collect* **BEN***'s body.)*

**CHIEF MCCLELLAND.** Good shot! Okay, he's dead. That's another one for the fire.

*(The* **CHIEF** *walks over to a glowing pile of burning bodies. He sighs loudly and stares into the fire.)*

Poor bastards. Hey is that Ernie Caldwell? Hey Vince, is this Ernie Caldwell?!

**VINCE.** *(Offstage.)* Yep! Shot him this morning.

**CHIEF MCCLELLAND.** Damn it. I guess I'll have to call his wife, Lucinda.

*(A* **ZOMBIE***'s hand explodes from the pile and reaches toward the* **CHIEF***.)*

AHH!

*(The* **CHIEF** *fires his rifle at the burning* **ZOMBIE***. The arm collapses. The* **CHIEF** *looks at the corpse.)*

Hey, Vince! Is that Lucinda Caldwell?

**VINCE.** Yep, shot her this morning.

**CHIEF MCCLELLAND.** You did a piss-poor job of it! What a mess!

*(***VINCE** *returns, dragging what appears to be* **BEN***'s body.)*

**VINCE.** Here's the one from the window. Looks like there was a group holed up in there. It's a damn shame.

**CHIEF MCCLELLAND.** If only we got here sooner. Maybe we could have saved them from these bastards.

*(The* **CHIEF** *kicks* **BEN***'s corpse.)*

**VINCE.** Well, I looked around some and I got a theory...

**CHIEF MCCLELLAND.** Knock it off! Never mind that. It don't matter now. Get back to it.

> (**VINCE** *exits. The* **CHIEF** *leans down and pokes at* **BEN***'s corpse.*)

Poor bastard. If only...

> (*Fade to black.*)

**[MUSIC CUE NO. 02]**

## Scene Three

*(A cemetery with several gravestones of different sizes. American flags are scattered amongst them. A tall stone stands in the back.)*

*(**BARBRA** enters, holding a funeral arrangement in the shape of a cross.)*

*(She looks around and smiles.)*

**BARBRA.** They ought to make the day the time changes the first day of summer. It's eight o'clock and it's still light out. Hmm. Lot of good the extra daylight did us. It'll be midnight by the time we get home to Pittsburgh. Right, Johnny?

*(**BARBRA** looks over her shoulder.)*

Johnny?

*(**BARBRA** looks out into the cemetery.)*

Johnny. Johnny!

*(**JOHNNY** pops out from behind the tall gravestone and grabs **BARBRA**.)*

**JOHNNY.** Barbra!

*(**BARBRA** screams. **JOHNNY** giggles.)*

**BARBRA.** Johnny!

**JOHNNY.** Come on! Loosen up, sis. We got anymore of that candy?

**BARBRA.** No, you're jumpy. No more candy until the ride back.

**JOHNNY.** Aw.

**BARBRA.** Show some respect.

**JOHNNY.** I'm just having a little fun! You really think I wanna blow Sunday on a scene like this?

**BARBRA.** Well if it really bugged you Johnny, you wouldn't do it. All Mother wants...

**JOHNNY.** You sound like Mother.

> (**BARBRA** *gasps, offended.*)

All right, all right, fine. Let's just get this over with. Which one is it?

> (**JOHNNY** *steps in front of the tall gravestone.*)

**BARBRA.** The one you're stepping on!

> (**JOHNNY** *looks down.* **BARBRA** *glares at him. He shrugs.* **BARBRA** *pulls him off the grave.*)

Get off! Here.

> (*She hands him the arrangement.* **JOHNNY** *inspects the arrangement.*)

**JOHNNY.** Look at this thing. "We Still Remember." I don't. I don't even remember what the man looks like.

**BARBRA.** Johnny, it takes you five minutes.

> (**BARBRA** *snatches the arrangement from* **JOHNNY.**)

**JOHNNY.** Yeah. Five minutes to put the wreath on the grave and six hours to drive back and forth. Besides, where's the one from last year? We spend good money on these things and every time we come back...it's gone!

> (**BARBRA** *places the arrangement on the grave.*)

**BARBRA.** I think you complain just to hear yourself talk!

**JOHNNY.** Look who I have to talk to. "They ought to make the day the time changes the first day of summer." It's like talking to a bowl of skim milk.

> (**BARBRA** *ignores* **JOHNNY** *and prays.* **JOHNNY** *puts on a pair of driving gloves. He's impatient.*)

Hey. Come on, Barb. Prayin's for church.

**BARBRA.** I haven't seen you in church lately.

**JOHNNY.** There's not much sense in my going to church. Do you remember one summer; we were small and we were out here. It was from right over there I jumped out at you from behind the tree. Grandpa got all excited and he shook his fist at me and said, "Boy, you'll be damned to hell!" Remember that?

> (**BARBRA** *continues to pray, ignoring* **JOHNNY**.*)*

**JOHNNY.** You used to really be scared here.

> (**JOHNNY** *sneaks up behind* **BARBRA**. *He puts his hands on her shoulders.)*

They're coming to get you, Barbra!

### [MUSIC CUE NO. 03]

> (**BARBRA** *squirms. A lightning flash illuminates an area where a lumbering* **GRAVEYARD ZOMBIE** *walks toward them. The flash ends and the* **GRAVEYARD ZOMBIE** *is plunged into darkness.)*

**BARBRA.** Johnny! Stop it!

> (**BARBRA** *continues to pray.)*

**JOHNNY.** They're coming for you, Barbra!

> (*Lightning flash. The* **GRAVEYARD ZOMBIE** *is a little closer to them now.* **BARBRA** *gets up.)*

**BARBRA.** Stop it! You're acting like a child.

**JOHNNY.** They're coming for you.

> (*Lightning flash. The* **GRAVEYARD ZOMBIE** *is slightly closer.* **JOHNNY** *points at him.)*

Look! There comes one of them now. I'm getting out of here.

> (**JOHNNY** *jokingly tries to hide behind* **BARBRA**.*)*

**BARBRA.** You're ignorant! He'll see you.

> (*Lightning flash. They look. The* **GRAVEYARD ZOMBIE** *is nowhere to be seen.* **JOHNNY** *stands up.)*

**JOHNNY.** Hmm. Maybe they're not coming to get you.

**[MUSIC CUE NO. 04]**

> (*The* **GRAVEYARD ZOMBIE** *jumps out from behind the tall gravestone and grabs* **BARBRA**.)

**GRAVEYARD ZOMBIE.** Arrrrgh!

> (**JOHNNY** *breaks in between them and struggles with the* **GRAVEYARD ZOMBIE**. **JOHNNY** *hits his head on a gravestone and falls behind it. The* **GRAVEYARD ZOMBIE** *looks at* **BARBRA**.)

> (*Chase music continues.*)

> (*A chase ensues.* **BARBRA** *and the* **GRAVEYARD ZOMBIE** *run into the audience.* **BARBRA** *falls and loses her shoes. She gets up and hides in the audience.* **GRAVEYARD ZOMBIE #1** *has vanished.*)

> (**GRAVEYARD ZOMBIE #2** *appears, played by a different actor in the same wig and costume.* **BARBRA** *escapes to another part of the theater.* **GRAVEYARD ZOMBIE #2** *disappears.*)

> (**GRAVEYARD ZOMBIE #3** *appears.* **BARBRA** *escapes him. She runs offstage, followed by* **GRAVEYARD ZOMBIE #3**.)

## Scene Four

(**BARBRA** *enters the farmhouse through the front door and slams it behind her. The chase music stops. She opens the door again. The chase music resumes. She shuts the door. The chase music stops again.*)

(*She locks the door and gathers herself. The house is tidy and clean.*)

(*She walks around the room and is startled by a taxidermy weasel.*)

### [MUSIC CUE NO. 05]

(**BARBRA** *attempts to use the phone, it fails. She looks outside, then to the stairs. She discovers a Dead Woman on the landing of the staircase. She approaches the woman.*)

BARBRA. Oh! Excuse me. Miss?

(**BARBRA** *taps the Dead Woman's shoulder. The body turns around, revealing its skeleton face.*)

### [MUSIC CUE NO. 06]

(**BARBRA** *shrieks.*)

### [MUSIC CUE NO. 07]

(*She unlocks and opens the front door to find* **BEN**, *who is backlit, holding a tire iron. They pause and stare at one another.*)

(*The* **GRAVEYARD ZOMBIE** *appears behind* **BEN**.)

GRAVEYARD ZOMBIE. ARGH!

(**BEN** *calmly elbows him in the face, grabs* **BARBRA**, *slams the front door, and locks it.*)

**BEN.** It's all right. Don't worry about him, I can handle him. There will probably be a lot more of them once they find out about us.

> (**BEN** *begins looking around the house.*)

My truck is outta gas. There is a pump out there. Is there a key? We can try to get outta here if we can get some gas. Is there a key?

> (**BEN** *picks up the phone.*)

I suppose you've tried this. Do you live here?

> (**BARBRA** *motions to the stairs.*)

## [MUSIC CUE NO. 08]

> (**BEN** *sees the Dead Woman.*)

Jesus. We have to get out of here. We gotta get to where there's some other people.

> (**BEN** *looks to* **BARBRA,** *she stares back.*)

Maybe we should take some food?

**BARBRA.** What's happening?

**BEN.** I'm just trying to make a plan here.

**BARBRA.** What's happening?!

> (*A loud groan from outside. They run to the window. There are now two* **ZOMBIES;** **GRAVEYARD ZOMBIE** *and* **HOUSE ZOMBIE.**)

**BEN.** There's two of them. Have you seen any more around here. I can take...

**BARBRA.** I don't know, I don't know. What's happening?

**BEN.** Really? I just told you there are two...

> (*More groaning from outside; a truck being smashed.*)

The truck!

> (**BEN** *opens the door. The* **GRAVEYARD ZOMBIE** *grabs him.*)

## [MUSIC CUE NO. 09]

*(They tussle out the door.)*

**BARBRA.** What's happening?

> *(The **HOUSE ZOMBIE** appears from the kitchen. He attacks **BARBRA**. They struggle.)*

> *(**BEN** returns and fights the **HOUSE ZOMBIE** with his tire iron. He knocks the **HOUSE ZOMBIE** to the floor.)*

**BEN.** Do you know a place down the road called Beakman's? Beakman's Diner? That's where I found that truck out there. I had jumped in to listen to the radio.

> *(The **HOUSE ZOMBIE** stands up.)*

A big gasoline truck crashed. Ten, fifteen of these things were chasing it.

> *(**BEN** lights a lighter. The **HOUSE ZOMBIE** stands still, looking at **BEN**.)*

It caught flame and they all backed away. That's how I found out they don't like fire.

> *(**BEN** pulls **BARBRA** behind him. He holds the lighter toward the **HOUSE ZOMBIE** and talks to **BARBRA**.)*

I looked back at the diner to see if there was anyone there to help me.

> *(**BEN**'s lighter goes out. The **HOUSE ZOMBIE** makes a move toward **BEN**. **BARBRA** screams. **BEN** lights the lighter again. The **HOUSE ZOMBIE** stops.)*

I realized I was alone.

> *(**BEN** focuses on the **HOUSE ZOMBIE** and backs him up, using the flame.)*

There were fifty or sixty of these things just standing there. Staring at me. I just stared back.

(*BEN turns off the lighter. The* **HOUSE ZOMBIE** *attacks.* **BEN** *expertly dispatches the* **HOUSE ZOMBIE,** *who falls behind the couch.* **BEN** *hits the* **HOUSE ZOMBIE** *with the tire iron multiple times.*)

I just wanted to kill them. Kill them all.

(*BEN carries the* **HOUSE ZOMBIE** *to the door and throws him outside. He uses the lighter to set fire to the* **HOUSE ZOMBIE** *corpse. Flames glow from outside.*)

That's when I noticed that the entire place had been surrounded.

(*BEN slams the door shut. Lightning flash reveals a* **ZOMBIE** *silhouette in every window.*)

I can still hear the man in that truck screaming.

**BARBRA.** We were riding to the cemetery... Johnny and me. We came to put a wreath on my father's grave.

(*BEN peaks out the window.*)

**BEN.** That fire is keeping those things at bay.

**BARBRA.** Johnny. He said, "Can I have some candy, Barbra." And we didn't have any.

**BEN.** That's a good story.

**BARBRA.** And he said, "Ooh, it's late. Why did we start so late." And I said, "Johnny, if you had gotten up earlier it wouldn't be so late." And then he said some things, and then I said more things, then he said some scary things...

**BEN.** Why don't you just keep calm.

**BARBRA.** And then a man grabbed me, and ripped... And my clothes...

**BEN.** I think you should just calm down.

(**BARBRA** *has another face-grabbing meltdown.*)

**BARBRA.** We have to go get Johnny! He's alone! You have to help me!

**BEN.** You're brother is dead.

**BARBRA.** No!

> (**BARBRA** *hits* **BEN. BEN** *slaps* **BARBRA** *in the face. She faints.*)

> **[MUSIC CUE NO. 10]**

> (*He grabs her as she falls. He is shocked. He looks around, guiltily.*)

> (**BEN** *gently puts* **BARBRA** *on the couch. He awkwardly loosens her jacket.*)

**BEN.** Do you want to listen to the radio?

> (**BEN** *goes to the radio upstage, turns it on.*)

## Scene Five

**RADIO.** *(Voice-over.)* Because of the obvious threat to citizens and because of the crisis, which is even now developing, this radio station will remain on the air, day and night.

> *(**BEN** searches the kitchen. He finds wood, nails, and a hammer to board up the windows.)*

*(Voice-over.)* At this hour, these are the facts as we know them: There is an epidemic of mass murder being committed by a virtual army of unidentified assassins. There is no apparent pattern or reason for the slayings. It appears to be a sudden, general explosion of mass homicide.

> *(**BEN** moves to a window and begins nailing boards over it.)*

*(Voice-over.)* Reaction of law enforcement officials is one of complete bewilderment. So far we have been unable to determine that any kind of organized investigation is yet underway.

> *(**BEN** moves to secure the other windows.)*

*(Voice-over.)* The scene is best described as mayhem and we advise you to keep listening to radio and television for any special instruction as this crisis develops further. We have some descriptions of the assassins. Eyewitnesses say they are ordinary people, while others say they appear to be in a kind of trance. So there is no authentic way for us to say who or what to guard yourself against.

> *(**BEN** listens carefully to the radio. He puts down his hammer and nails.)*

*(Voice-over.)* Your best bet is to trust no one. Even the most fragile creature could end up being a killer.

> *(**BEN** looks over at **BARBRA**, who is still unconscious. He begins to inspect her.)*

**RADIO.** *(Voice-over.)* Make sure to take caution around strangers who appear to be acting irrationally. Even seemingly unconscious victims can suddenly awaken and attack.

> *(A car horn honks continuously.* **BEN** *is startled. He looks out the window.)*

**BEN.** Those bastards!

> *(***BEN*** *walks to the door.)*

**RADIO.** *(Voice-over.)* It is recommended that you stay indoors, and not to leave your home for any reason.

> *(***BEN*** *opens the door, where the* **GRAVEYARD ZOMBIE** *and the* **DOOR ZOMBIE** *are waiting for him.)*

**GRAVEYARD & DOOR ZOMBIE.** Urgh!

> *(***BEN*** *quickly shuts the door.)*

**RADIO.** *(Voice-over.)* I repeat, do not leave your home for any reason. Make sure the door is locked.

> *(***BEN*** *locks the door.)*

*(Voice-over.)* And your windows are boarded up tight.

> *(***BEN*** *walks to the window he just boarded.)*

*(Voice-over.)* Use strong wood boards with good nails to keep the fiends at bay.

> *(***BEN*** *grabs the boards on the windows and gives them a test.)*

*(Voice-over.)* And for heaven's sake, don't leave a gap in the boards for the murderers to grab at you.

> *(A pair of* **ZOMBIE HANDS** *grabs at* **BEN** *through the gaps in the boards. He breaks himself free.)*

*(Voice-over.)* That would defeat the purpose entirely. Make sure to take short breaks to conserve your energy.

> *(***BEN*** *sits.)*

*(Voice-over.)* But don't rest too long. There's work to be done!

> *(**BEN** stands up.)*

*(Voice-over.)* Get busy finding useful items to defend yourself with. There will definitely be useful items in the tool shed.

> *(**BEN** runs to door and opens it. The **ZOMBIES** are still there. He closes the door.)*

*(Voice-over.)* ...But do not go outside.

**BEN.** Right.

**RADIO.** *(Voice-over.)* Look for any weapons or tools that you can use to survive this crisis. Check any cupboards or closets.

> *(**BEN** looks around.)*

*(Voice-over.)* Or even that awkward cubby under the stairs.

> *(**BEN** runs to the stairs.)*

*(Voice-over.)* Look for anything to defend yourself with. A bludgeoning weapon is reported to work against the fiends.

> *(**BEN** pulls out a baseball bat. He sets it down.)*

*(Voice-over.)* Then again, it may be possible to find something more deadly to fight with. An edged weapon, or something with a sharp point.

> *(**BEN** grabs an axe from the cubby. He sets it down.)*

*(Voice-over.)* Of course, when all else fails, there is always good ole American firepower.

> *(**BEN** pulls out a rifle. Music sting. He admires it and twirls it on his finger.)*

**BEN.** Groov–

**BARBRA.** NO!

(**BEN** *drops the gun and looks over to* **BARBRA**. *He walks to the radio and turns the volume down.*)

**BARBRA.** I just had the most awful dream. People were coming for me. From everywhere.

**BEN.** Calm down. Nobody smacked you.

(**BEN** *grabs some ladies shoes from out of the closet.*)

Here.

(*He walks over to hand them to* **BARBRA**, *who is still stunned. He puts them on her feet.*)

I found a gun and some bullets in there. This place will be boarded up pretty solid soon. We have a gun, food and a radio. We're doing all right.

(**BARBRA** *looks at him blankly.* **BEN** *grabs his gun.*)

## [MUSIC CUE NO. 11]

I don't know if you're hearing me, but I'm going to go upstairs now. If anything happens, I'll hear it from upstairs. I'll be back to reinforce the windows and doors. Everything is going to be okay.

(*He reaches out to touch her.*)

Okay? If you're okay, say nothing.

(**BEN** *looks at her. She stares blankly.*)

Terrific.

(**BEN** *turns the volume up on the radio and goes upstairs.* **BARBRA** *sits and stares blankly, listening to the radio.*)

## Scene Six

**RADIO.** *(Voice-over.)* Witnesses now reporting that the entranced murderers are killing and partially devouring their victims.

### [MUSIC CUE NO. 12]

(**BARBRA** *looks at the radio and slowly walks toward it.*)

*(Voice-over.)* Medical examination of victims' bodies show conclusively that the killers are eating the flesh of the people they kill.

(**BARBRA** *reaches the radio and is in a state of quiet panic.*)

*(Voice-over.)* And so this incredible story becomes more ghastly with each report. These reports have been verified as completely as is possible under the circumstances. This is happening. And so it appears no one is safe from this wave of mass murder. It's enough to make a person want to scream.

(*The door to the cellar opens, revealing* **TOM**. **BARBRA** *screams and runs.* **TOM** *grabs her.* **HARRY** *enters from the cellar, carrying a wrench.*)

**TOM.** Calm down! It's all right! Calm down!

**HARRY.** Pipe down, will ya!

(**BEN** *scurries down the steps. He points the gun at the intruders.* **TOM** *releases* **BARBRA**.)

Don't shoot! Here!

(**HARRY** *pulls out his wallet.*)

**BEN.** What?

**HARRY.** Oh. Nothing. A radio!

(**HARRY** *sits by the radio, dropping the wrench.* **BEN** *lowers the gun.*)

**BEN.** I thought you guys were one of them!

**TOM.** No, mister! We're from town!

**BEN.** And where have you been all this time?

**HARRY.** Downstairs in the cellar. It's the safest place!

**BEN.** You didn't hear the racket from up here?

**HARRY.** How were we supposed to know what's going on? It could have been those things for all we knew!

**BEN.** That girl was screaming. Surely you know what a girl screaming sounds like! Those things don't make any noise! Anybody would know that somebody needed help!

**TOM.** It's kind of hard to hear what's going on from down there.

**HARRY.** With the racket and screaming, it sounded like the place was being torn apart!

**BEN.** Now, wait a minute. You just got finished saying you couldn't hear anything from down there. Now you've said it sounded like the place was being ripped apart. It would be nice if you could get your stories straight, man.

> (**HARRY** *turns off the radio and gets into* **BEN**'*s face.*)

**HARRY.** Now you tell me! We luck into a safe place, and you're telling us we have to risk our lives just because somebody might need help, huh?

**BEN.** Yeah, something like that.

**TOM.** All right. Why don't we settle this...

**HARRY.** We came up. We're here! Now I suggest we all go back downstairs before any of those things find out we're in here!

**BEN.** They can't get in here.

> (**TOM** *inspects a boarded-up window.*)

**TOM.** You got the whole place boarded up?

**BEN.** Most of it. All but a few spots upstairs.

**HARRY.** You're insane. The cellar is the safest place!

**TOM.** *(To* **BEN.***)* His wife and kid are downstairs. The kid's hurt pretty bad.

**BEN.** Listen pal, I'm telling you. They CAN'T get in here!

### [MUSIC CUE NO. 13A]

*(A pair of* **ZOMBIE** *arms burst through the window and grab* **TOM.***)*

**TOM.** AAH!

**BEN.** I'm coming!

*(***BEN** *runs over and points his gun out the window. It is immediately grabbed by another pair of arms from outside. They struggle for it.)*

Damn it!

*(***TOM** *breaks free and grabs the hammer* **BEN** *used to board the windows.* **TOM** *hammers the* **ZOMBIE** *hands relentlessly. The hands bend and twist.* **BEN** *finally fires the gun. The* **ZOMBIE** *arms retract.)*

**TOM.** Nice shot! So all we have to do is shoot them in the stomach.

### [MUSIC CUE NO. 13B]

*(The arms come back and grab* **TOM.** **BEN** *aims his rifle through a lower slat and fires. The arms retreat.)*

**HARRY.** Ouch. Right in the Lyndon Johnston!

**TOM.** Great, so now we know. All we have to do is shoot them in the...

### [MUSIC CUE NO. 13C]

*(The arms grab* **TOM** *again and start choking him.* **BEN** *and* **HARRY** *try to free him.* **BEN** *aims at the fiend's head and fires. The* **ZOMBIE** *groans and the hands stiffen and retreat.)*

**BEN.** All we have to do is shoot them in the head.

**HELEN.** *(Offstage. From downstairs.)* Harry? Harry!

> *(**HELEN** enters from the cellar.)*

What's going on?

**BEN.** *(To **HELEN**.)* Ma'am. It's all right now.

**HARRY.** All right? You're nuts. Damn it, Helen! Get back downstairs!

**HELEN.** Well, somebody has his big boy pants in a knot. So all that screaming was from that woman...

> *(**HELEN** points at **BARBRA**.)*

**BEN.** So you could hear everything!

**HELEN.** Of course. She sounded a little...

> *(**HELEN** makes a crazy motion.)*

**HARRY.** Helen, we're going downstairs.

**HELEN.** Harry Cooper, you are thicker than a one dollar shake. Karen needs a doctor and soon. I'll look after her, you stay upstairs!

**HARRY.** Damn it, Helen!

**HELEN.** We may not enjoy living together, but dying together isn't going to solve anything. It was lovely meeting all of you.

> *(**HELEN** exits to the cellar.)*

**BEN.** She told you, Cooper.

**HARRY.** Listen. Those things are going to be in every window and door in this place!

**BEN.** We've just got to board this place up good. We'll be safe.

**HARRY.** No! We've got to get down in the cellar.

**BEN.** But we have everything we need up here.

**HARRY.** And we can take all that important stuff DOWNSTAIRS! For crying out loud, buddy! Are you high on the reefer? You got a million windows up here! They could come in from anywhere.

**BEN.** Well go on and get down in your cellar! Get out of here!

**HARRY.** Fine! And I'm taking her with me!

> (**HARRY** *points to* **BARBRA**, *still staring off into space on the couch.*)

**BARBRA.** ...

**HARRY.** On second thought. You keep her.

**BEN.** You keep your hands off her; and everything else that's up here too. Because if I stay up here, I'm fighting for everything up here; the radio and the food, everything!

**HARRY.** *(To* **TOM**.*)* The man's insane. He's insane! We've got to have food down there! We've got a right!

**BEN.** Is this your house?

**HARRY.** I know it isn't yours!

> (**BEN** *moves toward* **HARRY**. *He stops when* **JUDY** *peeks her head out from the cellar.*)

**JUDY.** Tom? Can I come up now?

**TOM.** Uuhh.

**BEN.** *(To* **TOM**.*)* You going down there with him?

**TOM.** Wellll.

**HARRY.** *(To* **TOM**.*)* Or you gonna let those things get her?

**TOM.** Uuhh.

**HARRY.** Listen; I got a kid down there. I couldn't bring her up here; with those things just outside!

**BEN.** Well you're her father: If you're stupid enough to go die in that trap, that's your business. However, I am not stupid enough to follow you. It's too bad for the kid that her old man is so stupid.

**HARRY.** Stupid? You are calling me stupid?! What's stupid is your stupid plan to stay in this stupid place! Stupid!

**TOM.** Mr. Cooper, If we stick together, we could fix it up real good. There's lots of places we can run to from here.

**HARRY.** Yeah! Like...THE CELLAR! Cripes!

> *(**HARRY** pulls **JUDY** into the room and steps into the cellar door.)*

**BEN.** Get the hell down in the cellar. You can be the boss down there; I'm boss up here!

**HARRY.** Bunch of yo-yos.

> *(**HARRY** slams the door and boards it up. He descends the stairs.)*

**TOM.** This is my girlfriend, Judy.

**BEN.** I'm Ben.

**JUDY.** Who's that?

**BEN.** That's... That's umm. You know, I never caught her name.

> *(**JUDY** sits beside **BARBRA**.)*

**JUDY.** Hi there. I'm Judy. What's your name?

> *(**BARBRA** starts to cry.)*

**BARBRA.** JOHNNY!

> *(**JUDY** awkwardly gets up and moves away from **BARBRA**.)*

**TOM.** How's Karen?

**JUDY.** She's not looking so good. She needs help. Poor little girl. I'm gonna look around, see if I can find anything for her.

> *(**JUDY** exits through the kitchen.)*

**BEN.** I still don't understand how you people didn't hear us down there.

**TOM.** It was really muffled.

> *(**HARRY** and **HELEN** can be clearly heard from downstairs.)*

**HELEN.** *(Offstage.)* What are you doing down here?

**HARRY.** *(Offstage.)* Damn it, Helen! Keep your voice down! They can hear you!

> *(**BEN** glares at **TOM**. **TOM** smiles sheepishly at **BEN**.)*

**HELEN.** *(Offstage.)* Do any of them know why we're being attacked?

**HARRY.** *(Offstage.)* Some kind of mass murder. The radio says to stay in...

**HELEN.** *(Offstage.)* They have a radio!

>               (**JUDY** *races back in from the kitchen.*)

**JUDY.** I found a TV in the other room. Somebody help me with it.

>               (**BEN** *follows* **JUDY** *into the kitchen.*)

**HELEN.** *(Offstage.)* They have a TV! Take the boards off that door and get up there!

**HARRY.** *(Offstage.)* Wait a god damn minute!

**HELEN.** *(Offstage.)* Go! Now!

>               (**BEN** *and* **JUDY** *enter, rolling in a television set.* **BEN** *adjusts the antennae while* **JUDY** *plugs it in.*)

**BEN.** Let me know when you see something.

>               (*Sounds of Harry prying away the boards can be heard from inside the cellar door. It swings open to reveal* **HARRY**.)

**HARRY.** I decided to come back. Oh, you found a television set.

**BEN.** Shut up!

**TOM.** I think we almost got something!

**HARRY.** *(To* **BARBRA**.*)* Now you better watch this and try to understand what is going on. I don't want anyone's life on my hands.

**BEN.** I don't want to hear anything more from you, mister. If you stay up here, you take orders from me! And that includes leaving the girl alone!

**JUDY.** It's on, it's on!

**HARRY.** There's no sound. Play with the rabbit ears.

### [MUSIC CUE NO. 14]

*(Everyone sits. Lights slowly cross-fade to reveal a news desk. A **NEWS ANCHOR** gives a report.)*

**ANCHOR.** Incredible as these reports may seem, it is not a result of mass hysteria.

**HARRY.** Mass hysteria?! Do they think we're imagining all this?

**BEN.** SHUT UP!

## Scene Seven

**ANCHOR.** The wave of murder that is sweeping the eastern third of the nation is being committed by creatures who feast upon the flesh of their victims. The public is being asked not to leave their homes for any reason. I repeat, do not leave your homes for any reason.

> *(A **HAND** holding a cue card abruptly comes out from the darkness. The **ANCHOR** grabs it.)*

This just in, leave your homes immediately and get to a rescue center as quickly as possible by any means necessary.

> *(A second cue card appears in the **ANCHOR**'s face very abruptly from the other direction.)*

This just in. News out of Washington. Why are space experts being consulted on an Earth-bound emergency? Rumors abound that the Venus satellite, purposefully destroyed by NASA recently, was carrying high levels of radiation.

> *(A third cue card sneaks slowly into the shot from below. The **ANCHOR** looks at it warily. He reads from the card.)*

Earlier today, our man in Washington caught the Chairman of the Joint Chiefs of Staff and his Chief Scientific Advisor leaving a meeting.

> *(The **HAND**, having fixed the **ANCHOR**'s hair, grabs the cards back.)*

Nancy!

## Scene Eight

*(Enter a* **REPORTER** *walking alongside a* **SCIENTIST** *and a* **GENERAL**. *They walk through the audience.)*

**REPORTER.** You're coming from a meeting regarding the Venus probe?

**GENERAL.** Yes, that was the subject of the meeting.

**REPORTER.** Do you feel like there's a connection...

**SCIENTIST.** There is a definite connection. A definite connection.

**GENERAL.** Aahh, uumm, nooo, no.

**REPORTER.** So, the radiation caused these mutations?

**SCIENTIST.** It was extremely high levels of radiation.

**GENERAL.** Now, um, wait a minute. I'm not certain that's the case at all.

**REPORTER.** So the military's viewpoint is the radiation is not the cause of the mutations.

**GENERAL.** Well, um, I can't speak for the entire military. But I disagree with this gentleman's comments.

**SCIENTIST.** But I just showed you the...

**GENERAL.** Rest assured that we are doing all that we can.

**SCIENTIST.** There is a definite connection as far as I am concerned.

**GENERAL.** Not proved! Not proved.
*(To the* **SCIENTIST**.*)* We had decided to say that it's not proved yet.

**SCIENTIST.** So much high-level radiation!

**GENERAL.** Professor! Please! Now if you'll excuse us, we are late for our next meeting.

**SCIENTIST.** What meeting?

**GENERAL.** Get in the car!

**SCIENTIST.** What meeting?

*(The* **GENERAL** *grabs the* **SCIENTIST**'s *arm and pulls him offstage.)*

**REPORTER.** Uncertainty, here in the nation's capital. Now, let's join Bill Cardill, who filed this report from Butler County, Pennsylvania.

## Scene Nine

*(Lights down on Washington and up on Butler County. Sounds of a rustling crowd and the occasional gunshot are heard.* **BILL CARDILL** *stands ready.)*

**BILL.** I'm Bill Cardill, here in Butler County. I've recently returned from a search and destroy operation against the ghouls. I'm with Connor McClelland, the Chief of Police. Local law enforcement here are doing their part against the ghoulish menace.

*(**CHIEF MCCLELLAND** stands by uncomfortably, carrying a rifle.)*

**CHIEF MCCLELLAND.** *(To the offstage posse.)* Hey Dale! Put that thing all the way in the fire. We don't want it getting up again!

**BILL.** Chief! How are things on the front line?

**CHIEF MCCLELLAND.** Oh, things aren't going too bad. Men are taking it pretty good.

**BILL.** Chief, any advice for how the folks at home can protect themselves?

**CHIEF MCCLELLAND.** If you have a gun, shoot 'em in the head. That's a sure way to kill 'em. If you don't, get yourself a club or a torch. Beat 'em or burn 'em; they go up pretty easy.

**BILL.** So, if I was surrounded by six or eight of these things, would I stand a chance?

**CHIEF MCCLELLAND.** Sure. I'll show you. We've prepared a demonstration.

*(Lights up on **DEMO ZOMBIE**, who is tied to a post.)*

Wake up. Oh yeah, she's all messed up.

**BILL.** This may be too graphic for those at home.

**CHIEF MCCLELLAND.** You wanted to show what it's really like out here, Bill. Now, hold this?

*(The* **CHIEF** *hands* **BILL** *his rifle.)*

**BILL.** I've never really held a gun. I was raised pacifist.

**CHIEF MCCLELLAND.** Nobody's perfect. First off, square yourself to the target. Hold the gun like a man would. Just put one in her head and we'll toss her on the fire.

> *(Bang!* **BILL** *shoots and misses. There is a scream offstage.)*

Oooo, that's all right. Dale, you okay?

**DALE.** *(Offstage.)* No, no, I'm good, you just put a hole in my leather jacket!

**CHIEF MCCLELLAND.** Okay, he's fine. Give her another shot, Bill.

> *(***BILL*** *shoots twice more.* **DALE** *screams from offstage. The* **ZOMBIE** *is confused.)*

*(To the offstage posse.)* Is Dale okay? No? Put him in the fire.

**BILL.** Another one for the fire! Sorry I got excited.

**CHIEF MCCLELLAND.** That's all right, heck, fire is excitin'. Now Bill, you can do this, buddy. Just relax and squeeze the trigger.

> *(The* **DEMO ZOMBIE** *growls.* **BILL** *shoots and gets the zombie in the head. Its brain splatters on the wall behind him. Lights down on* **DEMO ZOMBIE.***)*

**BILL.** Wahoo! Yeah! That slowed him down.

**CHIEF MCCLELLAND.** He was tied up. Still, nice shot!

**BILL.** Well, maybe I should join the posse, Chief?

**CHIEF MCCLELLAND.** Don't quit your day job just yet, Bill.

**BILL.** I guess I'll just stick with my microphone.

**CHIEF MCCLELLAND.** Yeah.

**BILL.** So what's next for the posse?

**CHIEF MCCLELLAND.** We'll be into it all night; probably into the morning. We're working our way towards the rescue center in Willard and we'll team up with the National Guard over there.

**BILL.** We wish you godspeed, Chief.

**CHIEF MCCLELLAND.** Whatever. *(He exits.)*

**BILL.** This is Bill Cardill, WIIC TV-11 news.

> *(Blackout.)*

**ANCHOR.** *(Voice-over.)* That was Bill Cardill, earlier today. Stay tuned to WIIC TV-11 for breaking news on the horrible events that have transpired these last few hours.

**[MUSIC CUE NO. 15]**

## Scene Ten

*(Lights up on the gang at the TV. Where* **JUDY** *was,* **HELEN** *now sits.* **BEN** *turns off the television.)*

**BEN.** Willard, I saw a sign that said Willard when I came in here.

*(***TOM** *enters from kitchen.)*

**TOM.** It's only about seventeen miles from here.

**BEN.** It's obvious our best move is to try to get out of here. We have that truck. We can get some gas, we can get out of here.

**TOM.** There's a pump near the shed.

**BEN.** I know, that's why I pulled in here, but it's locked.

**HARRY.** Please! How are you even going to get over to that pump?!

**HELEN.** He said the rescue stations have doctors and medical supplies. If we can get Karen there, we could get help for her.

**HARRY.** The cellar is the safest place!

**BEN.** The cellar is a death trap!

*(***HARRY** *grabs the axe.* **BEN** *grabs his gun.* **TOM** *grabs a baseball bat. Everyone freezes in a standoff.)*

## [MUSIC CUE NO. 16]

**HARRY.** You bastard!

**HELEN.** Harry!

**TOM.** All right, now. We just need to figure this thing out.

**BEN.** Fine. Then what's it going to be?

*(***BEN** *lowers his gun.)*

All right, listen. I'm going to make my way to that truck. It's the only way.

*(The others slowly lower their weapons.)*

**BEN.** Helen, why don't you go down and get...what's her name. Judy? You tell Judy to come up here, and you stay with the kid, all right?

(**HELEN** *goes downstairs.*)

We need to find something to distract those things.

**HARRY.** Oh, sure. We'll just go down to the cellar and grab some bottles or jars. We can make Molotov cocktails. Heck, there's a big can of kerosene down there! We can just set them all on fire.

**TOM.** That's not a bad idea.

**HARRY.** It's a horrible idea! We could be safe downstairs!

(**JUDY** *pops her head out of the cellar door.*)

Instead, you two would rather waste time making Judy down there look for bedspreads or sheets to tear up into strips.

**JUDY.** I'll see what I can find.

**TOM.** I'll look for the bottles.

(**JUDY** *goes downstairs.*)

**HARRY.** No!

**BEN.** Wait. Maybe Cooper's right. I'm not so sure about this plan.

**HARRY.** Thank you.

**BEN.** We still need to find the key to that gas pump.

**HARRY.** Yeah right, key to the gas pump. Like that key ring downstairs labeled "key to the gas pump."

**BEN.** Key to the gas pump? That might be the key to the gas pump!

**TOM.** Key to the gas pump. Comin' up!

(**TOM** *goes into the cellar.*)

**BEN.** We can toss the cocktails from a window upstairs. Meantime, a couple of us can go out and try to get the gas and come back for the rest of the people.

**HARRY.** But that'll leave a door open somewhere.

**BEN.** That's right. It better be this door. It's closer to the truck.

>     (**TOM** *comes from the cellar with a box and a key ring.*)

**TOM.** Look! I found these fruit jars in the cellar, just like Mr. Cooper said. And I found the key to the gas pump, all thanks to Mr. Cooper.

**HARRY.** Shut up!

**BEN.** I'm not really used to the truck. I found it abandoned.

**TOM.** I can handle the truck, no sweat.

**BEN.** You're it, then. You and I will go. Cooper, you can go upstairs and toss the cocktails from there. After we leave, you'll have to hustle back down here to lock this door. After we get the gas and get back into the house, then we'll worry about getting everyone into the truck. Now let's move.

>     (**HARRY** *takes the box and they all head for the kitchen.* **JUDY** *enters with a blanket and scissors.* **TOM** *sits on the couch with* **BARBRA**. **JUDY** *smiles and sits.*)

### [MUSIC CUE NO. 17/18]

**TOM.** You always have a smile for me. I don't know how you can smile like that all the time.

**JUDY.** Tom, are you sure we're doing the right thing, Tom?

**TOM.** What, about leaving here? It's what the television told us to do.

**JUDY.** I don't know.

**TOM.** Everything will be all right when we get to that rescue station. I promise.

**JUDY.** I wish I could do more to help.

**TOM.** Judy, you're my rock. When the time comes, I know I can count on you.

>     (**JUDY** *holds* **TOM** *close. They kiss sweetly.*)

*(They pull away and look back at* **BARBRA**. **BARBRA** *doesn't move. They hard-core make out. )*

*(***BEN** *and* **HARRY** *enter with the box of jars and kerosene.* **BEN** *holds a makeshift torch.* **TOM** *and* **JUDY** *pull apart.* **HARRY** *points to* **BARBRA**.*)*

**HARRY.** We better get her downstairs.

**JUDY.** Right. *(To* **BARBRA**.*)* We have to go downstairs now.

*(***BARBRA** *looks to* **BEN**.*)*

**BEN.** She's all right. You have to go downstairs now just for a little while until we get back. Then we can all leave.

**BARBRA.** Oh, I'd like to leave, yes.

*(***BARBRA** *and* **JUDY** *go downstairs.* **BEN** *joins* **TOM** *at the front door.* **TOM** *hands* **BEN** *a hammer.* **HARRY** *takes the box of Molotov cocktails upstairs.)*

**BEN.** Good luck.

*(***JUDY** *comes back upstairs and watches from the cellar door.)*

*(Yelling.)* Are you ready upstairs?

**HARRY.** *(Offstage yelling.)* I'd rather be downstairs in the cellar!

**BEN.** *(Yelling.)* Okay, drop 'em.

*(We hear the sounds of breaking glass and fire.)*

**[MUSIC CUE NO. 19]**

*(The flames outside can be seen through the windows of the house.* **HARRY** *runs down the stairs.)*

**HARRY.** Hold on, let me check!

*(***HARRY** *looks out the window.)*

## Scene Eleven

**HARRY.** Go ahead! Go on!

> (**BEN** *and* **TOM** *open the door and run out.* **HARRY** *looks out the window.*)

> (*Video:* **BEN** *and* **TOM** *running out the door.* **TOM** *fights off ghouls as he gets into the car.* **BEN** *stands by with shotgun [Approx. 1:08 of the film].*)

> (**HARRY** *pulls his head up.*)

Hey, they're doing real good! Those two make a pretty good team.

**JUDY.** I'm going with them!

> (**JUDY** *runs for the door.*)

**HARRY.** Get back in the cellar!

**JUDY.** No!

> (**JUDY** *runs out the door.* **HARRY** *chases* **JUDY**.*)

**HARRY.** Judy come back.

> (*He looks out the window.*)

> (*Video:* **JUDY** *running out of the house [Approx. 1:09:20].*)

> (**HARRY** *pulls his head up. He starts to panic. He flutters about the living room.*)

Oh, my god. Oh my god.

> (**HARRY** *runs around the room.*)

Harry, stick to the plan – lock the door.

> (**HARRY** *locks the door.*)

Oh, my god! Oh my god! Calm down.

> (**HARRY** *looks at the weasel, picks it up.*)

What is this a weasel? Who would do this? This animal is too small to taxidermy...

> (**HELEN** *enters from the cellar.*)

**HELEN.** Harry? What's going on?

**HARRY.** Judy ran outside like an imbecile!

**HELEN.** You should have stopped her!

**HARRY.** You should have stopped her down there!

**HELEN.** I can't be in two places at one time. What's going on?

> (**HARRY** *looks out the window.*)
>
> (*Video:* **JUDY** *gets in the truck [Approx. 1:09:30].*)
>
> (**HARRY** *pulls his head up.*)

**HARRY.** She got in the truck!

**HELEN.** Ugh, Judy is an idiot!

**HARRY.** Thank you! I can't stand her. Her voice is so annoying.

**HELEN.** I know. (**HELEN** *imitating* **JUDY**.) "Tom, are we doing the right thing, Tom?"

**HARRY.** I know! And she's so tall and gangly

**HELEN.** Nothing wrong with being tall.

**HARRY.** And her face!

**HELEN.** All right enough, look outside!

> (**HARRY** *looks out.*)
>
> (*Video: The truck driving to the pump [Approx. 1:10:30].*)
>
> (**HARRY** *looks in.*)

**HARRY.** They're doing it! They're driving it! Thank god Tom was here to drive the truck that Ben drove here!

> (**HARRY** *looks out.*)
>
> (*Video:* **BEN** *puts torch on grass,* **TOM** *throws gas on torch, truck catches on fire [Approx. 1:11:00].*)
>
> (**HARRY** *looks in.*)

**HELEN.** Well?

**HARRY.** Um, I can't say it's going well... I mean, there's fire involved now, that might work in their favor.

*(Flash of lights and an explosion sound.* **HARRY** *looks out.)*

*(Video: The truck completely on fire [Approx. 1:12:00].)*

*(***HARRY*** *looks in.)*

**HELEN.** What is it?

**HARRY.** They're all dead.

**HELEN.** All of them?

**HARRY.** Yes, get in the cellar.

**HELEN.** Oh my god, are you sure? What about the truck?

**HARRY.** Especially the truck. It's pretty gruesome. They're all dead and those things are coming for us, now get in the cellar!

**HELEN.** I have to see!

**HARRY.** Helen, this is no sight for a decent woman to see.

**HELEN.** Please, Harry. I'm a grown woman. How bad could it be?

### [MUSIC CUE NO. 20/21]

*(***HELEN*** *looks out. Lights up outside the house to reveal* **TOM** *being disemboweled by* **ENTRAILS ZOMBIE 1** *and* **ENTRAILS ZOMBIE 2**. *They pull out* **TOM***'s entrails and eat them.* **TOM** *is still alive, and he reaches toward* **HELEN**.*)*

**TOM.** Kill me.

*(She looks away. Lights down on* **TOM**.*)*

**HELEN.** I wasn't ready for that.

*(Banging on the door scares them both.)*

**BEN.** *(Offstage.)* Let me in!

**HELEN.** That sounds like Ben.

**HARRY.** Oooo, those monsters. They're so tricky! Go in the cellar!

**BEN.** *(Offstage.)* Cooper! Cooper! Unlock the door!

**HARRY.** Aahh, I uuhh...

(**HARRY** *pushes* **HELEN** *into the cellar.*)

**HELEN.** For Christ's sake!

(**BEN** *knocks at the window.* **HARRY** *hides up against the wall.*)

**BEN.** Cooper, I can see you!

**HARRY.** Damn it!

(**HARRY** *runs to the door, opens it, and he and* **BEN** *push* **ZOMBIES** *back outside.* **BEN** *slams the front door shut and locks it. They step back from the door and see that it's secure.*)

(**BEN** *punches* **HARRY** *multiple times and holds him down on the couch.*)

**BEN.** I should drag you out there and feed you to those things!

## Scene Twelve

(**BEN** gets off of **HARRY**. **HELEN** and **BARBRA** enter from the cellar.)

**BARBRA.** It's ten minutes to three, we don't have long to wait now. Ten to three is closer to three than quarter to three, but, then again, it's closer than half past two!

(They pause and stare at **BARBRA**.)

**HELEN.** (Dryly.) I'm so glad those monsters spared you, honey.

**BEN.** Do you know anything about this area at all? I mean, is Willard the closest town?

**HELEN.** I dunno. We were just trying to get to a motel before it got dark.

**BEN.** Let's get that car of yours.

**HELEN.** Seems like we ran a long way.

**HARRY.** Forget it. It's at least a mile. You gonna carry that kid a mile through those things?

**BARBRA.** Johnny has the keys.

**BEN.** I can carry the kid. What's wrong with her? How did she get hurt?

**HELEN.** One of those things grabbed her.

**HARRY.** Bit her on the arm.

(**BEN** stares at **HELEN**.)

**HELEN.** What's wrong?

**BEN.** Who knows what kind of diseases those things carry.

**HARRY.** Who knows what kind of diseases you carry!

(**HARRY** looks to **HELEN** for acknowledgement. **HELEN** shakes her head.)

**BARBRA.** You won't find the keys.

**HARRY.** Nobody's talking to you!

**BEN.** Shut up! Let's hear the next broadcast...

(The power goes out in the house.)

Is there a fuse box downstairs?

**HARRY.** I dunno, I...

> (**BEN** *goes downstairs.*)

Helen. I have to get that gun!

**HELEN.** Haven't you done enough?

**HARRY.** Two people are dead already on account of that guy.

> (**BEN** *enters.*)

It's not the fuses. It's the power lines.

### [MUSIC CUE NO. 22]

> (*A pair of undead arms bust through the window.* **BEN** *and* **HELEN** *run to secure the house.* **BEN** *drops his gun.* **HARRY** *runs to the cellar door, sees the gun, picks it up, and points it at* **BEN**.)

Go ahead! Go ahead! You wanna stay up here now? Helen get in the cellar.

**HELEN.** You get in the cellar!

**HARRY.** Get in the cellar, now!

**HELEN.** You get in the cellar!

**BEN.** Nobody's getting in that cellar!!

> (**BEN** *lunges for* **HARRY**, *but* **HARRY** *throws* **HELEN** *in front of him.* **BEN** *pushes her aside, grabs the gun, and shoots* **HARRY** *in the belly.* **HARRY** *falls into the basement.* **HELEN** *backs up against the window.*)

**HELEN.** Harry!

> (**ZOMBIE** *arms come through the front window and grab* **HELEN**. **BARBRA** *jumps up to help.*)

**BARBRA.** I'll help you.

> (**HELEN** *breaks free. The window boards break, and* **BARBRA** *ends up jumping directly into the arms of* **ZOMBIE JOHNNY**. *He grabs* **BARBRA**, *and along with the* **GRAVEYARD ZOMBIE**, *they disembowel her in the window.*)

(**BEN** *tries to help* **BARBRA,** *but all he manages to grab are her intestines as she's pulled through the window.* **BEN** *grabs her guts and looks at them with deep sadness as they slip through his hands.*)

Goodbye blonde woman... This... This is disgusting...

(**ZOMBIES** *break through the big window!* **GRAVEYARD ZOMBIE** *and* **ZOMBIE JOHNNY** *enter.* **HELEN** *runs downstairs.* **BEN** *gets ready to fight.*)

**BEN.** Come on! Let's go!

(*Fight scene.* **BEN** *does away with the two* **ZOMBIES** *handily.* **BEN** *runs to the front door.*)

Is that all you got?!

(*Sound effects:* **ZOMBIE** *chorus moans.*)

(*Blackout.*)

**[MUSIC CUE NO. 23]**

## Scene Thirteen

*(Lights up on cellar steps.* **HELEN** *slowly descends the stairs. There are muffled sounds of* **BEN** *fighting the ghouls upstairs.)*

**HELEN.** Karen? Karen?

*(***HELEN*** *stands on the landing. She looks into the cellar to find her daughter.)*

*(A small pool of light shows* **KAREN** *hovering over* **HARRY***'s corpse. It appears that she is holding her father.)*

Karen. My baby.

*(***HELEN*** *approaches* **KAREN** *and embraces her.)*

## [MUSIC CUE NO. 24]

*(***KAREN*** *turns around to reveal her face. It's covered in blood as she chews on a piece of* **HARRY***'s body.* **HELEN** *freezes.)*

My baby!

*(***KAREN*** *drops* **HARRY** *and reveals a garden trowel. She grabs her mother and slashes at her violently.)*

AAHH!

*(***KAREN*** *pulls* **HELEN***'s body into the darkness.)*

*(***BEN*** *enters from the staircase, carrying the rifle. He slams the door shut and barricades it behind him. He takes a long, tired breath and makes his way down to the landing.)*

**BEN.** Helen?

*(***BEN*** *sees* **HARRY***'s corpse. The sounds of moaning as* **KAREN***, along with reanimated* **HARRY** *and* **HELEN***, emerge from the darkness.)*

*(The three* **COOPER ZOMBIES** *tumble back into the darkness.)*

(**BEN** *slumps onto the basement landing. He listens as the* **ZOMBIES** *from upstairs bang on the door.*)

(**BEN** *grabs his rifle and reloads it as the noises from upstairs swell. He cocks the rifle and sits on the floor, ready for any attacker.*)

Hhmm. Nice cellar. Looks pretty safe.

(*Blackout.*)

**[MUSIC CUE NO. 25**

## Scene Fourteen

*(The sounds of dogs barking, birds chirping, and murmured voices in the distance. A helicopter passes overhead.)*

*(Gunshots are heard as* **CHIEF MCCLELLAND** *and* **VINCE** *enter and approach the outside of the house.)*

**VINCE.** You see that truck back there?

**CHIEF MCCLELLAND.** Looks like somebody had a cookout. *(Yelling offstage.)* Nick. Steve. You wanna get out in that field and build me a bonfire. Let's check out the house.

> *(***BEN** *slowly enters from the basement door. He cautiously looks outside the window.)*

**VINCE.** There's something in there. I heard a noise.

> *(***BEN** *looks out the window.* **VINCE** *raises his gun.)*

**CHIEF MCCLELLAND.** All right, Vince hit him in the head. Right between the eyes.

> *(***VINCE** *shoots* **BEN** *in the head. He runs over to collect* **BEN**'s *body.)*

Good shot. Okay, he's dead. That's another one for the fire.

> *(The* **CHIEF** *walks over to a glowing pile of burning bodies. He sighs loudly, staring into the fire.)*

Poor bastards. Hey is that Ernie Caldwell? Hey Vince, is this Ernie Caldwell?!

**VINCE.** *(Offstage.)* Yep! Shot him this morning.

**CHIEF MCCLELLAND.** Damn it. I guess I'll have to call...

> *(The* **CHIEF** *notices* **LUCINDA**'s *arm rising out of the pile.)*

Hey, Lucinda!

*(The* **CHIEF** *fires his rifle at* **LUCINDA**. *The arm collapses. The* **CHIEF** *looks at the corpse.* **VINCE** *enters, dragging what appears to be* **BEN**'s *body.)*

**VINCE.** Yep! Shot her this morning!

**CHIEF MCCLELLAND.** You did a piss-poor job. What a mess!

*(***VINCE** *throws* **BEN**'s *corpse on the fire.)*

**VINCE.** Here's the one from the window. Looks like there was a group holed up in there. It's a damn shame.

**CHIEF MCCLELLAND.** If only we got here sooner. Maybe we could have saved them from these bastards.

*(The* **CHIEF** *kicks* **BEN**'s *corpse.)*

**VINCE.** Well, I looked around some and I have a theory.

**CHIEF MCCLELLAND.** Never mind that. It don't matter now. Get back to it.

**VINCE.** Chief, hear me out! I reckon they probably spent the night fighting for their lives upstairs. Then, they got overrun and this poor fella tried to hide in the cellar, but they got in there as well. He fought them off and then came upstairs and that's where I shot him.

**CHIEF MCCLELLAND.** Wait. Are you saying this fella was a human when we shot him?

**VINCE.** Maybe.

**CHIEF MCCLELLAND.** He was a ghoul! I could tell by the way he was holding his gun! Anyhow, it doesn't matter. He's in the fire now.

**VINCE.** All I'm saying is maybe if these folks had chose to just stay in the cellar in the first place, things might have played out different. The cellar is the safest place.

**CHIEF MCCLELLAND.** The cellar is always a death trap.

**VINCE.** Think about it, if he...

**CHIEF MCCLELLAND.** Knock it off. It don't matter now. Get back to it.

*(***VINCE** *exits. The* **CHIEF** *leans down and pokes at* **BEN**'s *corpse.)*

CHIEF MCCLELLAND. Poor bastard. If only...they had all hid in the cellar. Maybe then, they would've survived.

*(Fade to black.)*

**[MUSIC CUE NO. 26]**

## Scene Fifteen

*(Lights up to the house at the standoff.)*

*(**HARRY** holds the axe. **BEN** holds his gun. **TOM** has a baseball bat. Everyone freezes in a standoff.)*

**HARRY.** You bastard!

**HELEN.** Harry!

**TOM.** All right, now. We just need to figure this thing out.

**BEN.** Fine. Then what's it going to be?

*(**HARRY** lowers his weapon.)*

**HARRY.** Listen to me. The more noise and commotion we make up here, the more of those things we attract. Come down to the cellar. I swear, nothing can get past that door. Eventually, those things will go away, and someone will rescue us. My daughter. My poor Karen. She's hurt. I can't bring her up here. Please.

*(**HARRY** begins to weep. The others lower their weapons.)*

**TOM.** He's got a point. We've been safe down there till now.

*(**BEN** looks at the others. He nods.)*

**BEN.** All right then. The cellar.

*(They all file downstairs. **BEN** takes a hard look at **HARRY**, who appears grateful.)*

You better be right about this.

### [MUSIC CUE NO. 27]

*(**BEN** exits down the stairs. **HARRY** looks around the house one last time. He smiles and closes the cellar door behind him.)*

*(Blackout.)*

## End of Act I

# ACT II

## Scene One

### [MUSIC CUE NO. 28]

> (**HARRY, TOM, BEN, BARBRA,** *and* **HELEN** *stand on the landing of the cellar stairs, surrounded by darkness.*)

**BEN.** I can't see a thing.

**HARRY.** Tom, get the lights.

> (**TOM** *hits a switch and the cellar set is revealed. There is a workbench on one end of the room. On the other side, a bedsheet hung on a clothesline blocks off a corner of the space. Everyone walks downstairs.*)

**TOM.** See. It's not so bad down here.

**BARBRA.** Oh, I like it.

**BEN.** Yeah, it's a real destination. Let's move. Tom, go get that radio.

> (**TOM** *heads back upstairs.*)

**HARRY.** Hold on. I give the orders down here. Tom, go get that radio!

**HELEN.** Will you two stop it!

> (**TOM** *opens the door, and* **GRAVEYARD ZOMBIE** *lunges at him.* **TOM** *pushes* **GRAVEYARD ZOMBIE** *out. He pins down the door.*)

**BEN.** Hold on!

(**BEN** *places the gun on the workbench.* **HARRY** *grabs the gun as* **BEN** *grabs the plank for the door.* **HARRY** *points the gun at* **BEN**.)

**BEN.** We don't have time for this!

**HARRY.** You're right. I order you to secure that door.

(**TOM** *struggles to keep the* **GRAVEYARD ZOMBIE** *out.*)

**TOM.** Gentlemen, please. If we just work together.

**HELEN.** For god sakes!

(**HELEN** *grabs the plank from* **BEN** *and heads upstairs.*)

**BEN.** You're a lot tougher holding that rifle, aren't you.

**HARRY.** You said it yourself. You're boss upstairs. I'm boss down here.

**BARBRA.** It's true. You did say it.

(**TOM** *pushes the* **GRAVEYARD ZOMBIE** *out and puts the plank in the door brace.* **HELEN** *comes downstairs.*)

**HARRY.** We need a leader. Someone who's not afraid to make tough decisions.

**HELEN.** There! It's secure.

**HARRY.** Helen. Cover these two while I check the door. If they move, shoot them.

(**HARRY** *gives* **HELEN** *the gun and runs partway up the stairs.* **HELEN** *cocks the gun, unloading the bullets. She collects the bullets and puts them in her pocket.*)

(**HARRY** *turns to see* **HELEN** *handing the gun to* **BEN**.)

Woman! Have you lost your mind!

**HELEN.** No, but obviously you have.

(**HELEN** *runs behind the curtain.*)

**BEN.** Don't worry she's got all the bullets.

**HARRY.** Perfect!

**TOM.** It is perfect. Don't you see. Now you both have the power. Whenever we need to use the gun, you both have to come to a consensus. Like at the United Nations.

(**BEN** *and* **HARRY** *groan in disgust.*)

**HARRY.** Bunch of pinko garbage. Helen, give me those bullets.

(**HARRY** *runs behind the curtain.*)

**BEN.** Tom, think about this. If we need to use that gun, we won't have time to discuss it.

**TOM.** All I know is we're safe now. The only thing that can hurt us...is us. This system protects us from each other.

(**JUDY** *comes out from behind the curtain.*)

**JUDY.** Mr. Cooper just kicked me out of there. He said behind the curtain is off-limits.

**BEN.** Damn it! Cooper!

(**HARRY** *comes out with a shovel and defends the curtained area.*)

**HARRY.** Not one step closer! You want to play U.N.? Fine! This is my country. No one goes past this curtain.

**BEN.** No way. You have the first aid kit back there. What if someone gets hurt.

**HARRY.** You'll just have to ask for my help. Or make a trade.

**BEN.** This is childish. Fine. I get the workbench. How's that?!

(**BEN** *moves to the workbench.*)

**BARBRA.** Oh fun. I'm the Queen of the workbench.

**TOM.** Gentlemen, this is really unnecessary!

**JUDY.** Wait! Tom, what do we get?

**TOM.** Judy, we don't need to get anything.

**JUDY.** We call the staircase.

(**JUDY** *runs to the stairs.*)

**HARRY.** No way! You can't do that! That should be common space.

> (**JUDY** *sees a jug of water at the foot of the stairs. She grabs it.*)

**JUDY.** And we have the water.

**BEN.** What?!

**TOM.** Calm down, everyone. We all get access to the water.

**JUDY.** As long as we're on diplomatic speaking terms.

**TOM.** Judy, what's got into you?

**JUDY.** Get up here, Tom. The staircase needs you.

> (**TOM** *walks onto the stairs. Everyone relaxes.*)

There. That's better.

**TOM.** Well, if that's what it takes for peace. Maybe we should set some ground rules.

**BARBRA.** Where's the bathroom?

> (*Everyone looks at each other.*)

**HARRY.** Well, it's not going to be in my territory. Do it over there.

**BEN.** Cooper, there's no privacy over here.

**BARBRA.** I have to go pretty bad.

> (**BEN** *finds a bucket. He points to the stairs.*)

**BEN.** Take this. Go under the stairs.

> (**BARBRA** *takes the bucket and goes under the stairs.*)

**TOM.** Come on! That's not fair.

**HARRY.** You took the stairs. Not under the stairs.

**JUDY.** Just go back as far as you can, all right.

**TOM.** All right, wait. If this is going to be a real democracy, we should vote where we dump our waste. I say, not under the stairs. It's a health hazard as well as being gross. All in favor?

*(**JUDY** and **TOM** vote "Ay.")*

Opposed?

*(**BEN** and **HARRY** vote "Nay.")*

**BEN.** Motion carried. We pee under the stairs.

**JUDY.** What? It was two to two?!

**HARRY.** It was two to one. Each country gets one vote.

*(**HARRY** and **BEN** awkwardly high five.)*

**BEN.** I have to admit, this is working out.

**HARRY.** See! What did I tell you.

### [MUSIC CUE NO. 29]

*(The blanket curtain is backlit to show a silhouette of **HELEN** sitting on the bed.)*

*(Suddenly, **KAREN**'s shadow sits upright. She's holding a garden trowel.)*

*(Note: the others cannot see what is happening behind the curtain.)*

The cellar is the safest place. I said it from the very beginning. Didn't I, Mister "The Cellar is a Death Trap"?

*(**KAREN** begins stabbing **HELEN**. Blood splatters against the curtain.)*

**HELEN.** *(Offstage.)* Harry!

**HARRY.** Okay! I'm sorry, Helen! She told me not to say I told you so, but you know what? I told you so! Man, it feels good just saying it!

*(**KAREN** starts to dismember and eat **HELEN**'s corpse. **KAREN** rips **HELEN**'s spinal column out of her body.)*

**BEN.** Helen? Is everything all right back there?

**HARRY.** Don't you worry about my area. My family is none of your concern. Helen?

*(**HARRY** ducks behind the curtain. In silhouette, we see **HARRY** witness **KAREN***

> *chewing on* **HELEN**'s *spinal cord. He returns to the others. The curtain silhouette light fades.)*

**HARRY.** Everything's fine. Just...teenagers.

**BEN.** Tell us what happened.

**HARRY.** It's fine, it's fine. My daughter's fine. We're all fine!

> *(***KAREN*** throws* **HELEN**'s *head and spine over the curtain. It lands in front of everyone. They all scream!)*

It's my daughter. It happened within my border. I'll deal with it.

**BEN.** She just threw your wife's central nervous system at us! What are you going to do? Spank her?

> *(***TOM*** starts to walk off the stairs.)*

**TOM.** Gentlemen...

**BEN.** Get your ass back on those stairs!

> *(***BEN*** points the gun at* **TOM**.*)*

**TOM.** That gun's not even loaded.

**BEN.** I will push this gun through your face if you don't back up! Move!

> *(***TOM*** retreats to the stairs.* **BEN** *approaches* **HARRY**.*)*

Give me a bullet. Let me end it.

**HARRY.** I should do it. She's my daughter. Please. Let me do this.

> *(***BEN*** hesitates, then gives him the gun.)*

**BEN.** All right. I'm sorry, Cooper.

> *(***HARRY*** begins to load the gun with several bullets.)*

If you shoot her in the head, she'll go quick. One shot. You won't need that many rounds.

### [MUSIC CUE NO. 30]

> *(***HARRY*** shoots* **BEN**.*)*

**BEN.** Damn it, Cooper!

> (**BEN** *falls.* **HARRY** *turns to* **KAREN** *and shoots her.* **TOM** *and* **JUDY** *begin tearing off the boards to the door, trying to escape.* **HARRY** *looks up at them. They stop.* **TOM** *walks down the stairs.)*

**TOM.** Harry, I know this system hasn't worked out quite as planned...

> (**HARRY** *shoots* **TOM**.)

**JUDY.** Tom! No!

> (**JUDY** *runs to* **TOM**. **HARRY** *shoots* **JUDY**. **HARRY** *is alone.)*

> (**BARBRA** *cautiously enters from under the stairs.)*

**BARBRA.** I'm done peeing now. You shot them all?

**HARRY.** Yep.

**BARBRA.** Are you going to shoot me, too?

**HARRY.** Probably.

**BARBRA.** Then I'm going to go.

**HARRY.** I'll walk you out.

> (*They walk up the stairs to the door.)*

**BARBRA.** Nice meeting you. Sorry about your family. Be careful here, it's a little slippery. Well, goodbye.

**HARRY.** Goodbye.

> (**BARBRA** *opens the door.)*

**BARBRA.** Oh. Johnny.

### [MUSIC CUE NO. 31]

> (*Two* **ZOMBIE** *arms pull her off, and* **HARRY** *closes the door. He replaces the brace, then heads down the stairs, where he hears the sound of* **BEN** *laughing.)*

**BEN.** Cooper. Cooper.

**HARRY.** What?

**BEN.** I told you...the cellar is a death trap.

> (**BEN** *dies.* **HARRY** *sits.*)
>
> (*Slowly, the bodies of the others begin to reanimate.* **HARRY** *loads his gun.*)
>
> (*Blackout. Sound of gunshots and* **ZOMBIE** *moans.*)

**[MUSIC CUE NO. 32]**

## Scene Two

*(Outside the farmhouse. Morning. The sounds of dogs barking, birds chirping. A helicopter passes overhead.)*

*(Gunshots are heard as* **CHIEF MCCLELLAND** *and* **VINCE** *enter and approach the outside of the house.)*

**CHIEF MCCLELLAND.** Looks like somebody had a cookout. *(Yelling offstage.)* Nick. Steve. You wanna get out in that field and build me a bonfire. Let's check out the house.

**VINCE.** There's something in there. I heard a noise.

*(**HARRY** slowly enters from the cellar door. He has the rifle.)*

**HARRY.** I'm alive. I did it.

*(**HARRY** cautiously looks outside the window. **VINCE** raises his gun.)*

**CHIEF MCCLELLAND.** All right, Vince hit him in the head. Right between the eyes.

**HARRY.** No. Wait!

*(**VINCE** fires. **HARRY** falls. Lights down on the farmhouse.)*

**CHIEF MCCLELLAND.** Good shot! Okay, he's dead. That's another one for the fire.

*(**VINCE** walks toward the house. The **CHIEF** walks to the bonfire.)*

Poor bastards. Hey is that Ernie Caldwell? Hey Vince, is this Ernie Caldwell?!

**VINCE.** *(Offstage.)* Yep! Shot him this morning.

**CHIEF MCCLELLAND.** Damn it. I guess I'll have to call his wife, Lucinda.

*(The **CHIEF** looks closely at another corpse.)*

Hey, Vince! Is this Lucinda Caldwell.

**VINCE.** *(Offstage.)* Yep, shot her this morning.

> *(The **CHIEF** bends to look at the corpse.)*

*(Offstage.)* Twice! I wouldn't want to do a piss-poor job!

**CHIEF MCCLELLAND.** Smart ass. What a mess!

> *(**VINCE** enters.)*

**VINCE.** Looks like there was a group holed up in the cellar.

**CHIEF MCCLELLAND.** How many?

**VINCE.** Four women. One Caucasian male, pretty young. A black fella and the weasely looking guy I shot.

**CHIEF MCCLELLAND.** Damn shame.

**VINCE.** It is.

**CHIEF MCCLELLAND.** Wonder what happened.

**VINCE.** Looks like they all turned on each other. Multiple gunshots everywhere.

**CHIEF MCCLELLAND.** No wonder. There was no real leadership down there.

**VINCE.** How can you tell?

**CHIEF MCCLELLAND.** You said it yourself. A young kid or some weasely looking guy leading a bunch of women?

**VINCE.** There was the black fella.

> *(**CHIEF** laughs.)*

What? It's 1968.

**CHIEF MCCLELLAND.** Come on, now. To survive a situation like that, a group needs an All-American leader type. Someone who fits the part.

**VINCE.** You mean a white guy?

**CHIEF MCCLELLAND.** That's not what I said. Don't be smart. Clean up that house.

> *(**VINCE** leaves. The **CHIEF** looks into the fire.)*

If only they had a whi...All-American leader type. Maybe then, they would've survived.

> *(Blackout.)*

**[MUSIC CUE NO. 33]**

## Scene Three

*(Lights up to the house at the standoff.* **BEN** *is missing.)*

**HARRY.** You bastard!

**HELEN.** Harry!

**TOM.** All right, now. We just need to figure this thing out.

> *(***WHITE BEN*** [played by* **CHIEF MCCLELLAND***] enters from upstairs.)*

**WHITE BEN.** Hey, gang!

## [MUSIC CUE NO. 34]

**ALL.** Ben!

> *(***WHITE BEN*** lowers his weapon. He speaks calmly and assertively as he walks downstairs.)*

**WHITE BEN.** Let's figure this thing out. Obviously, we have our differences. All of us are strangers in a strange house.

But I believe we have more in common than we do not. We certainly have a common enemy. So what say, we put aside all this and try to get this house in order. Agreed?

**ALL.** Yeah. Sure. Sounds great.

**WHITE BEN.** Swell. Tom, I want you to make sure all of the windows and doors are secure. Barbra, be a doll and help him, will you?

> *(***BARBRA*** giggles.)*

**TOM.** Will do.

> *(They spring into action and eventually exit to the cellar.)*

**WHITE BEN.** Harry, I know that you have strong opinions about the cellar, but we're going to go ahead and stay up here.

**HARRY.** But the cellar is...

**WHITE BEN.** The safest place. I agree. I didn't want to say it in front of the others. I was hoping that you could take charge of things in the cellar. Make sure it's ready for when we need it most.

**HARRY.** I guess I can go down there and fix things up, but shouldn't we go down there now?

**WHITE BEN.** We should go down there now, it's true, but let's face it. Not everyone in this house is mature and composed enough to be stuck down in a dark, crowded cellar for a long period. I mean, that kid? Those girls?

> *(They both have a chuckle.* **WHITE BEN** *puts a hand on* **HARRY**'s *shoulder.* **HELEN** *rolls her eyes.)*

You're my number one man, Cooper. If something should happen to me...god forbid.

**HARRY.** No, we're all going to be all right. You can count on me.

**WHITE BEN.** I know it.

> *(***HARRY*** *heads downstairs.* **WHITE BEN** *approaches* **HELEN**.*)*

Helen, I have something special for you to handle.

**HELEN.** Stuff it.

**WHITE BEN.** Excuse me?

**HELEN.** Sorry. I guess some of us are not mature and composed enough to be stuck here with you.

**WHITE BEN.** You didn't think I was talking about you?

**HELEN.** I am one of "those girls."

**WHITE BEN.** On the contrary, you are the mature, composed person I was speaking about.

**HELEN.** Please.

**WHITE BEN.** Helen, I mean it. I need you...to be a part of this. Will you help me?

> *(***WHITE BEN** *looks deeply into* **HELEN**'s *eyes. She begins to melt.)*

**HELEN.** What is it you need me to do?

**WHITE BEN.** Make us a pot of coffee. It's going to be a long night.

>       (**WHITE BEN** *walks up the stairs.*)

**HELEN.** I'm nobody's secretary, mister. You've got the wrong girl.

**WHITE BEN.** I'm sorry, you're right. You're mature and composed. Go look after your daughter.

>       (**HELEN** *heads for the cellar.* **WHITE BEN** *calls to her from the stairs.*)

Send that young, pretty one up to make the coffee. I'll be up here if anyone needs me.

>       (**WHITE BEN** *climbs the stairs.* **HELEN** *fumes and leaves for the cellar as* **HARRY** *and* **TOM** *come upstairs.*)

**HARRY.** Look, kid. Don't get upset.

**TOM.** Don't call me kid, old man.

**WHITE BEN.** What's going on down there?

>       (**TOM** *and* **HARRY** *start complaining about each other.* **BARBRA** *enters and starts yelling as well.*)

Knock it off!!

>       (*The men stop as* **BARBRA** *keeps yelling randomly. She notices them and then stops, coyly.*)

Do I have to come down there?! Do I?

>       (*They mumble "No."*)

All right. One at a time. Tom, what's this about?

**TOM.** I had an idea I wanted to tell you, but Harry wanted to take credit for it.

**HARRY.** That's not true!

>       (*They all start fighting.*)

**WHITE BEN.** Hey!!

*(Silence.)*

**WHITE BEN.** What's the idea?

**TOM.** The truck you came in on. We just need to find the key to the gas pump out there and we can fill it and take it to safety.

> *(**HARRY** enthusiastically raises his hand.)*

**WHITE BEN.** Harry.

**HARRY.** I found this key ring downstairs! It's labelled "key to the gas pump".

> *(**HARRY** proudly displays the keys. **TOM** gives **HARRY** the cut-eye. **JUDY** enters from the cellar.)*

**WHITE BEN.** Nice work, Harry. Get a plan together and let me know what you come up with. New girl!

> *(He points to **JUDY**.)*

**JUDY.** I'm not new. I was just downstairs.

**WHITE BEN.** I'm waiting on that coffee.

> *(**WHITE BEN** exits upstairs. **TOM** scolds **JUDY**.)*

**TOM.** Judy! Come on!

**JUDY.** I just got here!

> *(She runs into the kitchen.)*

**HARRY.** Here's the plan. There's some bottles downstairs. We can make Molotov cocktails and set them all on fire.

**TOM.** Molotov cocktails sounds kind of communist. He may not like that.

> *(**HELEN** screams from downstairs. **BARBRA** opens the cellar door.)*

**HARRY.** What's happening?!

**BARBRA.** I think they're playing Farmer's Garden. Helen's face is the garden and Karen's digging a lot.

**HARRY.** What?!

**BARBRA.** Oh. Now she's eating stuff from the garden.

(**WHITE BEN** *enters from upstairs.*)

**WHITE BEN.** Boys! What have you got for me?

**HARRY.** My daughter has turned into one of them. She's killing Helen.

**WHITE BEN.** Harry, I thought I put you in charge of the cellar?

**HARRY.** She's eating her face!

**WHITE BEN.** That's unacceptable! Get down there and fix it! Tom, where are we with the truck.

(**HARRY** *grabs an axe and heads downstairs.* **TOM** *is shaken.*)

**TOM.** Um, well. Molotov cocktails?

**WHITE BEN.** Too communist. Look, I'll cover you. Fill the tank, drive over here and pick me up in five minutes. I'm still waiting on that coffee, new girl!

**JUDY.** (*Offstage.*) Coming!

**TOM.** Are you sure you can cover me?

**WHITE BEN.** Maybe I should get Harry for this.

**TOM.** No!

**WHITE BEN.** Here we go. Three, two, one! Go!

(**TOM** *runs out the front door.* **ZOMBIES** *groan.* **JUDY** *enters with a coffee tray.*)

**JUDY.** Tom! No!

(*She runs after him.*)

**WHITE BEN.** Leave the coffee!

(**JUDY** *hands the coffee to* **BARBRA** *and runs out the door.*)

Barbra, I'm going to be a minute. Keep that coffee warm.

(**WHITE BEN** *exits upstairs. Screaming outside.* **WHITE BEN** *walks downstairs.*)

Never mind, they're already dead. I'm going down to the cellar to check on Cooper. Don't let anyone in here.

(**WHITE BEN** *takes a coffee and drinks. He smiles and raises the cup to* **BARBRA**.)

**WHITE BEN.** That's my girl.

(**BARBRA** *giggles.* **WHITE BEN** *heads downstairs.* **ZOMBIE** *arms burst through the windows.* **BARBRA** *tries to assume a professional demeanor.*)

**BARBRA.** I'm sorry. You'll have to come back later. He's very busy. There's coffee.

### [MUSIC CUE NO. 35]

(*Blackout. Sound of moaning and the door being smashed.* **BARBRA** *screams.*)

## Scene Four

> (**BLACK CHIEF MCCLELLAND** *[played by* **BEN***]* *and* **VINCE** *approach the house.*)

> (**WHITE BEN** *slowly enters from the cellar.*)

**VINCE.** There's something in there. I heard a noise.

> (**WHITE BEN** *looks out the window.* **VINCE** *raises his gun.*)

**BLACK CHIEF MCCLELLAND.** All right, Vince hit him in the head. Right between the eyes.

**WHITE BEN.** Don't shoot. I'm a person.

> (**BLACK CHIEF MCCLELLAND** *snatches the rifle from* **VINCE**.*)

**BLACK CHIEF MCCLELLAND.** Hold your fire! By Golly! Looks like you survived a pretty rough night, mister.

**WHITE BEN.** Some people are just born luckier than others, I guess. Let me talk to the man in charge.

**BLACK CHIEF MCCLELLAND.** I'm the man in charge.

> (**WHITE BEN** *laughs.*)

**WHITE BEN.** Seriously. And get me a coffee and an Aspirin. My head is killing me.

> (**BLACK CHIEF** *shoots* **WHITE BEN**. *He walks over to the fire.* **VINCE** *follows.*)

**VINCE.** What the heck!

**BLACK CHIEF MCCLELLAND.** You heard him. He had a bite on his head.

**VINCE.** He said he had a headache.

**BLACK CHIEF MCCLELLAND.** Tomato, Tom-ah-to. It's a damn shame.

**VINCE.** Chief, you may have just shot an innocent man. That was a very rash decision.

**BLACK CHIEF MCCLELLAND.** Sometimes you have to make rash decisions, kid. That's part of being a man.

**VINCE.** My mother said you should never make rash decisions.

**BLACK CHIEF MCCLELLAND.** I guess your mother wasn't much of a man, was she? I suppose you think your mother would do a better job running things here? Heck, if it was up to you, we'd let the women take over everything!

**VINCE.** Maybe. What? It's 1968.

**BLACK CHIEF MCCLELLAND.** Don't be smart. You want to know what it's like being led by women? Go clean up that house!

(**VINCE** *exits.*)

**VINCE.** (*Offstage.*) Maybe if more women were in charge, I wouldn't have to clean up that house!

**BLACK CHIEF MCCLELLAND.** Women in charge! Right. Maybe then, they would've survived.

(*Blackout.*)

**[MUSIC CUE NO. 36]**

## Scene Five

*(Lights up to the house at the standoff.)*

*(**HELEN** and **BARBRA** are missing. The men are not holding weapons.)*

**HARRY.** You bastard!

**TOM.** All right, now. We just need to figure this thing out.

**BEN.** Fine. Where's my gun?

*(The men look around for their weapons.)*

**HARRY.** Wait a minute. Where are the girls?

**TOM.** Outside. There's fire everywhere.

*(**BARBRA** and **HELEN** enter from the front door. **HELEN** has the rifle and **BARBRA** is holding the axe and the baseball bat.)*

**HELEN.** Nice work, Barbra!

**BARBRA.** Oh thank you! I like helping.

*(The men are dumbfounded. **HARRY** grabs the bat and axe from **BARBRA**.)*

**HARRY.** Are you crazy, woman?

**HELEN.** Calm down, Harry.

**HARRY.** Trusting your life with this vegetable!

**HELEN.** She has been worth a lot more than all three of you blowhards put together.

**HARRY.** We've been figuring things out!

**HELEN.** And while you've been figuring things out, we've made a perimeter of fire around the house.

**BARBRA.** They don't like fire.

**HELEN.** We kept them at bay with torches and used the wood and kerosene for the fire.

**BARBRA.** And then we cleaned up the yard.

**HELEN.** We noticed they've been using rocks and bricks from the yard as tools to smash windows.

**BARBRA.** And I got to make signs. They say "Survivors Inside."

**HELEN.** That way, none of us are mistaken for monsters when we're all rescued.

(*The three men stare, dumbly, at* **HELEN.**)

**BARBRA.** Good plan, huh?

(**BARBRA** *and* **HELEN** *high five.* **TOM** *goes to join in.*)

**TOM.** It is pretty sound.

(**HARRY** *hits* **TOM.**)

**BEN.** So I suppose we just sit around now and wait?

**BARBRA.** Yes. Maybe there is some candy in the house? That'll calm you boys down. You're jumpy.

**TOM.** Lady, I'm not jumpy. I'm worried. Where's Judy?

**BARBRA.** Did you just call me Lady?

(**BEN** *and* **HARRY** *back away.*)

**TOM.** I guess I did.

**BARBRA.** You don't know my name!

**TOM.** We weren't ever introduced!

**BARBRA.** I just helped save your life and you don't even know my name!

**HELEN.** Now, Barbra...

**BEN.** Barbra!

**TOM.** He didn't know your name either!

**BEN.** Tom...

**TOM.** It's true, he asked me earlier to introduce myself to you so we could figure out your name. He was feeling bad because he smacked you.

**BARBRA.** (*Realizing.*) Oh yeah! You smacked me!

(*Everyone looks at* **BEN.** **BEN** *gets hysterical.*)

**BEN.** Now, wait a minute. She was being hysterical. I had no choice.

(**BARBRA** *hits* **BEN** *the same way he originally hit her. He falls into her arms.*)

**BARBRA.** I had no choice.

*(She places* **BEN** *on the couch.)*

**HARRY.** Nice punch, lady!

**BARBRA.** It's Barbra! Bar-bra! They're coming to get you Barbra!

**TOM.** Excuse me! Barbra! Where is Judy?

**BARBRA.** She's taking first watch.

**TOM.** Judy! No!

> *(***TOM*** *runs out the door. There is a glow from the flames outside.)*

**HELEN.** Tom! Watch out for the flames!

> *(***BARBRA*** *looks out the door and describes what she's seeing. Sound effects accompany what she is describing.* **TOM** *starts screaming.)*

**BARBRA.** Tom's on fire. Now he's trying to find Judy. He found her.

> *(***JUDY*** *screams from offstage.)*

Judy's on fire. They're jumping and running. The house is on fire.

**HARRY.** Great! Nice job, ladies! Perfect plan! Come on, Ben!

> *(***BEN*** *grabs the axe and heads for the door.)*

**BEN.** Fine, let's clean up your idiot wife's mess.

**HARRY.** Don't you call my wife an idiot.

**BEN.** She married you didn't she!

**HELEN.** How is this my fault?!

**BEN.** Maybe if you would have shared this plan with us, we could have helped. Tom and Judy wouldn't be on fire right now. Idiot!

> *(***BEN*** *walks out the door.* **HARRY** *grabs the gun and chases him.)*

**HARRY.** You come back here! Nobody else calls my wife an idiot!

> *(***HARRY*** *exits. A gunshot blast and the sound of a struggle outside.)*

**BEN.** Cooper!

**HARRY.** Die, you bastard!

> (*Both men start screaming.* **BARBRA** *looks out the door.*)

**BARBRA.** They're on fire. Should we help?

**HELEN.** No. Get into the cellar. We'll be safe down there with Karen.

> (*They run to the cellar.*)

**BARBRA.** Good thinking, Helen. We girls need to stick together. Oh Karen, you're up.

> (*She locks the door. The sounds of* **KAREN** *killing* **HELEN** *and* **BARBRA** *are heard.*)
>
> (*Blackout.*)

**[MUSIC CUE NO. 38]**

## Scene Six

*(The* **CHIEF** *is beside the glowing pile of bodies.)*

**CHIEF MCCLELLAND.** What a mess.

*(***VINCE** *enters, dragging a body. He throws it on the fire.)*

**VINCE.** *(Out of breath.)* Looks like there was a group holed up in there. Half the house is burned down. Everyone was either burned up or eaten.

**CHIEF MCCLELLAND.** Damn!

**VINCE.** It's a shame. I looked around some and I have a theory.

**CHIEF MCCLELLAND.** Never mind that now!

**VINCE.** Chief, hear me out! It's like they barricaded themselves in with fire to wait for us. If they had just occupied those monsters longer, maybe we could have saved them in time?

**CHIEF MCCLELLAND.** Occupy? Like how?

**VINCE.** Someone could've sacrificed themselves for the group.

**CHIEF MCCLELLAND.** Ridiculous! Who the hell would sacrifice themselves?

**VINCE.** I would sacrifice myself for you.

**CHIEF MCCLELLAND.** That's nice.

**VINCE.** Would you...

**CHIEF MCCLELLAND.** Knock it off. It don't matter now. Get back to it.

*(***VINCE** *sadly exits. The* **CHIEF** *leans down and pokes at a corpse.)*

Sacrifice someone from the group. Maybe then, they would've survived.

**[MUSIC CUE NO. 39]**

## Scene Seven

*(Lights up to the house at the standoff.)*

*(**HARRY** holds the axe. **BEN** holds his gun. **TOM** has a baseball bat. Everyone freezes in a standoff. Music bump.)*

**HARRY.** Bastard!

**HELEN.** Harry!

**TOM.** All right!

**BEN.** Fine. When I first came upon that truck I drove here, those things were feeding on the driver. It made it easy for me to escape.

**TOM.** So if we throw a body out there we could wait out this mess and get rescued in the morning!

**HELEN.** One problem, we don't have any dead bodies just lying around here.

**BEN.** There's an old woman's corpse upstairs. But looks like those things already got to it. It won't do.

**HARRY.** We got her. *(Pointing to **BARBRA**.)*

**BARBRA.** Johnny?

**HARRY.** See? She could be dinner!

**BEN.** She stays. Maybe you should go out there for the greater good.

**HARRY.** I'm a father! Why don't you go out there?

**BEN.** I could. Or we could send out that sick kid of yours.

**HELEN.** Over my dead body.

**BEN.** Then we'd have two dead bodies.

**HELEN.** Why not send Judy out there, she's never around anyway.

**TOM.** Not my Judy.

**HELEN.** Well then, who? Me? I'm not sure they'd even eat me, I'm so bitter.

**HARRY.** Ain't that the truth.

*(They all argue.)*

**TOM.** Hey! Stop it. Listen. I go. I'm the youngest. Hell, I haven't even started my life, yet. I have nothing to lose.

**BEN.** Are you sure you want to do this, man?

**TOM.** Yeah.

### [MUSIC CUE NO. 40A]

I'm doing this for the group. The greater good. For the ones who died and the ones who can be saved, yet. For the optimistic future to preserve our glorious past. I do this for us, and if Judy were around, I'd do it for her.

> (**TOM** *walks out the door. He is eaten.* **BEN** *steps to the door.*)

**BEN.** Courage.

### [MUSIC CUE NO. 40A]

His sacrifice shows us we all have more to sacrifice. Tom inspired us to live bigger than we are and to die taller than we lived. I follow Tom for us. And if Barbra weren't so vacant, I'd do it for her.

> (**BEN** *walks out the door. He is eaten.* **HELEN** *steps to the door.*)

**HELEN.** Yes,

### [MUSIC CUE NO. 40A]

I'm a mother. Yes, my daughter needs me in the cellar, but I believe doing this will help her to live on with Judy, whom I just met.

Harry, you're a bastard and I don't do this for you. Try being a man and sacrifice yourself when I'm gone.

> (**HELEN** *walks out the door. Is eaten.* **HARRY** *steps to the door.*)

**HARRY.** Great. I gotta take orders in the last moments of my life.

### [MUSIC CUE NO. 40B]

I die the way I lived. Bastardly.

> (**HARRY** *walks out the door. Is eaten.*)

**[MUSIC CUE NO. 40B]**

(**BARBRA** *steps to the door and stares blankly at the audience. She opens the door and exits.*)

**BARBRA.** Johnny?

(**BARBRA** *is grabbed and eaten.*)

(*Beat.*)

(**JUDY** *comes upstairs, runs through the house and out the front door.*)

**[MUSIC CUE NO. 40C]**

**JUDY.** Tom!

(**JUDY** *is eaten.*)

(*Blackout.*)

**[MUSIC CUE NO. 40B]**

## Scene Eight

*(The* CHIEF *stands beside a glowing pile of bodies.)*

CHIEF MCCLELLAND. What a mess.

*(*VINCE *enters, dragging a body. He throws it on the fire.)*

VINCE. Well, here's the last one. *(Out of breath.)* Looks like there was a group holed up in there.

CHIEF MCCLELLAND. Ah, damn!

VINCE. Shame.

CHIEF MCCLELLAND. It is.

VINCE. Chief, I looked around some and I have a theory. I reckon one by one, all of those people volunteered to just walk out and get eaten by those things.

CHIEF MCCLELLAND. How did you figure that...?

VINCE. Never mind, they're in the fire now. They should have just assimilated with the undead.

CHIEF MCCLELLAND. That's disgusting, Vince.

VINCE. Chief, do you know what "assimilated" means?

CHIEF MCCLELLAND. Do you know what "assim-tilated" means?

VINCE. Convinced the ghouls they were ghouls too.

CHIEF MCCLELLAND. That's what I thought it meant. Knock it off! It don't matter now. Get back to it.

*(*VINCE *exits. The* CHIEF *leans down and pokes at a corpse.)*

If only they had...astimulated with the ghouls. Maybe then, they would've survived.

**[MUSIC CUE NO. 41]**

## Scene Nine

*(Lights up in the house at the standoff.)*

*(HARRY holds the axe. BEN holds his gun. TOM has a baseball bat. Everyone freezes in a standoff. Everyone speaks at the same time.)*

**HARRY.** You bastard!

**HELEN.** Harry!

**TOM.** All right!

**BEN.** Fine!

What's it going to be?

*(BARBRA stares blankly out the window.)*

**HARRY.** We go downstairs!

**BEN.** Upstairs!

*(As they all argue, BARBRA quietly opens the front door and exits. The lights come up outside the house. BRAIN ZOMBIE is sitting by himself, eating brains out of a human head. BARBRA appears.)*

**HARRY.** Hey! Why is the door open?

*(The group looks over to the front door.)*

**BEN.** Barbra? Barbra!

**TOM.** My god! She's outside! Look!

### [MUSIC CUE NO. 42]

*(They move over to the window and watch. BEN calls out the window.)*

**BEN.** Barbra! Get back in here! Now!

*(BRAIN ZOMBIE notices BARBRA and stands up. It growls and starts to stalk toward her. She stares blankly at the BRAIN ZOMBIE.)*

**BRAIN ZOMBIE.** Arrghh!

**BEN.** That's it. I'm going to get her!

(**BEN** *rushes out the front door.*)

**HELEN.** Wait! No!

**BRAIN ZOMBIE.** ARRGHH!

> (**BARBRA** *doesn't move.* **BARBRA** *whines loudly. She sounds like a* **ZOMBIE.**)

**BARBRA.** Ugghh.

**BRAIN ZOMBIE.** Arrghh.

**BARBRA.** Uuugh!

**HARRY.** Well, I'll be. It thinks she's one of them.

> (*The* **BRAIN ZOMBIE** *moans.* **BARBRA** *whines. They stand beside each other. It's almost peaceful.*)

**TOM.** I think she's on to something. If we act like the monsters, we could just walk right out of here.

> (*The* **BRAIN ZOMBIE** *turns away. He resumes chewing on the head.* **BEN** *sneaks over and grabs* **BARBRA.**)

**BEN.** *(Whispering.)* Come on! Let's go!

> (*The* **BRAIN ZOMBIE** *spins around and looks at* **BEN.**)

**HELEN.** Ben! Do what Barbra's doing!

**BEN.** What?

**BRAIN ZOMBIE.** Arrghh!

> (*The* **BRAIN ZOMBIE** *moves toward* **BEN.**)

**HARRY.** Act like the monsters!

> (**HARRY, HELEN,** *and* **TOM** *leave through the front door. The* **BRAIN ZOMBIE** *reaches toward* **BEN.**)

**BEN.** Uughh.

> (*The* **BRAIN ZOMBIE** *freezes.*)

**BRAIN ZOMBIE.** Uughh?

**BEN.** Uughh.

*(TOM, HARRY, and HELEN appear outside.)*

*(The BRAIN ZOMBIE hands the human head to BARBRA and motions for her to eat some brains.)*

**HELEN.** Look at that. Oh, that's nice.

**HARRY.** Christ.

**HELEN.** You never gave me a thing in your whole damn life!

**HARRY.** Stop talking. Act like them!

**HELEN.** I'm getting Karen. Our daughter? Remember her?

*(HELEN leaves. The BRAIN ZOMBIE looks at TOM, BEN, and HARRY.)*

*(Instantly, they all moan and shuffle like the undead. The BRAIN ZOMBIE groans louder and shakes the dismembered head in front of BARBRA.)*

**BEN.** *(Out of the side of his mouth.)* Barbra. Eat!

*(BARBRA takes the head and has a nibble. She chews slowly. Brain chunks roll down her chin.)*

**TOM.** Urggh. Way to go Barbra!

*(HARRY and BEN turn to TOM, still posing as ZOMBIES.)*

**BEN & HARRY.** Shut up! Urgghhhh!

**BRAIN ZOMBIE.** Muhhhhhhh…

*(The BRAIN ZOMBIE pushes the head toward BEN. BEN screws up his face. HARRY walks over to BEN. He quietly coaches him to eat the brain.)*

**HARRY.** Urrgh! Do it. Eat that brain.

**BEN.** *(Side of his mouth.)* Bluhhhh! Shut up, Cooper.

**BRAIN ZOMBIE.** Uurgh!

**BEN.** Okay! Okay! Uurgh!

(**BEN** *grabs the head and struggles to eat the brains. He tries to look happy as the* **BRAIN ZOMBIE** *watches him eat.*)

**BEN.** Ugh. Om nom nom nom!

**HARRY.** Urrghh! Ha, ha. Gross.

(*The* **BRAIN ZOMBIE** *turns to* **HARRY.** *He offers him the skull.* **HARRY** *looks at it and shakes his head.* **BEN,** *his mouth still full of brains, motions for* **HARRY** *to eat.*)

Okay. Here, I go. Gonna eat a brain.

(**HARRY** *cautiously tries to eat. He takes a sniff.*)

Yeah, I'm not going to eat this.

(**BEN** *spits out the brains.*)

**BEN.** Cooper!

## [MUSIC CUE NO. 43]

(*The* **BRAIN ZOMBIE** *attacks* **BEN.**)

**HARRY.** Arrghh! Let's get out of here while they eat Ben!

(**TOM** *goes to save* **BARBRA.** **BARBRA** *attacks* **TOM,** *biting at his neck.* **HARRY** *watches in horror.*)

Barbra, what are you doing?!

(**TOM** *escapes.* **BRAIN ZOMBIE** *follows.* **BARBRA** *turns to* **HARRY.**)

**BARBRA.** I'm coming to get you, Harry!

**HARRY.** You're not a monster!

**BARBRA.** What?

(**HARRY** *tries to escape, but runs into* **HELEN.**)

**HARRY.** Helen, get Karen! Barbra's gone crazy. We need to...

(**HELEN** *falls into his arms. She has a trowel in her back.*)

**HARRY.** Aaahh!

> *(**BARBRA** stalks. **HARRY** smiles and offers **BARBRA HELEN**'s head.)*

Om nom nom nom?!

> *(Blackout. **HARRY** screams.)*

**[MUSIC CUE NO. 44]**

## Scene Ten

*(The **CHIEF** stands by the pile of glowing bodies. He yells to **VINCE**, who is offstage.)*

**CHIEF MCCLELLAND.** What a mess. Hey Vince! We got reports that people have been trying to act like the undead to try to survive.

Ridiculous! Why didn't they just teach those things to be human again? Maybe then, they would've survived.

**[MUSIC CUE NO. 45]**

## Scene Eleven

*(In the farmhouse. **BEN, HARRY, BARBRA,** and **HELEN** gather around **UNDEAD JOHNNY.** **BARBRA** feeds **UNDEAD JOHNNY** some candy from a candy dish on the table.)*

**BARBRA.** You like that Johnny? Yes, Johnny loves candy!

*(**BARBRA** continues to stuff candies into **UNDEAD JOHNNY**'s mouth. He hardly chews them.)*

See! I told you he was okay.

**HELEN.** Wow. I think she's right. Good thing we saved him.

**HARRY.** Damn it. We need to ration these!

*(**HARRY** reaches for the candy dish and **UNDEAD JOHNNY** rips off his arm. Everyone screams. He begins to eat it.)*

*(Blackout.)*

**[MUSIC CUE NO. 48]**

## Scene Twelve

*(The* CHIEF *is by the fire.)*

CHIEF MCCLELLAND. What a mess. Hey, Vince! Looks like people are getting killed trying to teach the undead to be human. Ridiculous! If only they had used their god-given, constitutional right to arm themselves to the teeth. Maybe then, they would've survived.

*(Blackout.)*

**[MUSIC CUE NO. 49]**

## Scene Thirteen

*(Lights up on the standoff. Everyone is holding a different gun.* **HARRY** *has a tommy gun.)*

*(***BARBRA*** *has a grenade.* **TOM** *has a bazooka.* **HELEN** *has a laser gun.* **BEN** *has his rifle.)*

*(They all point and yell at each other.)*

*(Shots. Everyone dies but* **BARBRA***. She jumps up and down to celebrate and pulls the grenade pin.)*

**BARBRA.** Oops.

*(Blackout. Sound of explosion.)*

## Scene Fourteen

*(The* **CHIEF** *stands beside a glowing pile of bodies.* **VINCE** *enters and stands beside him.)*

**CHIEF MCCLELLAND.** What a mess! Hey Vi–!

**VINCE.** Yeah?

**CHIEF MCCLELLAND.** Sorry. I thought you were...never mind. What's the report?

**VINCE.** Well Chief, I looked around some and I have a theory.

**CHIEF MCCLELLAND.** Never mind that! It don't matter now! Get back to it.

**VINCE.** Hear me out, Chief! Seems like there was no way for these people to have survived. I thought about it, and the folks in there had no chance, whatsoever.

**CHIEF MCCLELLAND.** Vince, I know it seems that way, but I don't believe that.

**VINCE.** But how? A bunch of strangers, with nothing in common and no training, with all their different backgrounds and agendas. How could they survive?

**CHIEF MCCLELLAND.** By choosing to band together as a team. Exploiting each others' strengths and agreeing upon common goals. When folks work together, there's nothing they can't overcome.

**VINCE.** Chief, that's a load of horse shit. We don't live in that kind of world. I don't think it even exists.

*(**VINCE** exits. The **CHIEF** leans down and pokes at a corpse.)*

**CHIEF MCCLELLAND.** Wait. That's it. If they just lived in a world where people, despite their differences, worked together against the odds to reach a common goal. Maybe then, they would've... Wait a minute. That is a load of horse shit.

*(The* **CHIEF** *starts to walk away. He turns and sings.)*

### [MUSIC CUE: "WORK TOGETHER"]

**CHIEF MCCLELLAND.**
UNLESS...

## Scene Fifteen

*(Lights up to the house at the standoff.)*

*(**HARRY** holds the axe. **BEN** holds his gun. **TOM** has a baseball bat. They all start arguing.)*

**BEN.** Stop!

> *(**BEN** lowers his weapon.)*

I KNOW YOU'RE SCARED,
AND I AM AWARE,
THOSE THINGS AREN'T WHAT YOU FEAR.
WE CAN'T LET HATE, IDEALS OR DEBATE
BE WHY WE ALL DIE HERE.

**TOM.** Ben, what can we do?

> *(Music swells.)*

**BEN.**

LOOK AT OUR FOES
THEY ALREADY KNOW
THE POWER OF BEING ONE.
THEY CHOOSE TO AGREE
ONE BIG FAMILY
LET'S LEARN FROM WHAT THEY'VE DONE.

**TOM.**

HOW?

**HARRY.**

YEAH, HOW?

**HELEN, BARBRA & BEN.**

HOW?

**GRAVEYARD ZOMBIE 1.**

UGGHH...

**BEN.**

BY WORKING TOGETHER!

> *(The others look at each other in bewilderment.)*

**ALL.**

TOGETHER!

**HELEN.** It's a wonderful idea!

**BEN.**

I PUT MY TRUST IN EVERY ONE OF YOU.

**HELEN.**

THAT'S THE WAY IT SHOULD BE!

**HARRY.**

I USUALLY DON'T BUT TONIGHT I WILL TOO

**TOM.**

I SPEAK FOR JUDY
WHEN I SAY WE AGREE

**HELEN.**

LET'S POOL OUR KNOWLEDGE

**TOM.**

FROM THE FARM

**BEN.**

THE STREETS

**HARRY.**

AND COLLEGE.

**ALL.**

LET'S WORK TOGETHER

**BEN.**

LET'S STAY STRONG AND FIGHT

**ALL.**

LET'S WORK TOGETHER

**HARRY.**

SHOW THESE MONSTERS THAT
WE HAVE A RIGHT!

**BEN & HARRY.**

LET'S MAKE EACH AND EVERY MOANING BASTARD PAY
FOR EVERY LIFE AND HOME THEY TOOK AWAY
FORGET OUR PAST 'CAUSE TOMORROW IS TODAY

**ALL.**

LET'S WORK TOGETHER TONIGHT!

**TOM.**

WE ALL DO THE BEST THAT WE ARE ABLE!

**HELEN.**

THERE'S NO "I" IN "TEAM."

**BEN.**

EVERYONE BRINGS SOMETHING TO THE TABLE!

**BARBRA.**

EVEN ME!

*(Everybody else shakes their head "no.")*

**HARRY.**

LET'S OPEN THE FRONT DOOR

**BEN.**

IT'S TIME FOR THE LIVING TO SETTLE THE SCORE

**ALL.**

LET'S WORK TOGETHER

**BEN.**

LET'S KILL 'EM COLLECTIVELY.

**ALL.**

LET'S WORK TOGETHER

**HELEN.**

AND PUNCH 'EM ALL OUT LIKE MUHAMMAD ALI!

**ALL.**

STANDING SIDE BY SIDE THERE'S NOTHING WE CAN'T DO.
IF YOU GOT MY BACK I SWEAR I GOT YOURS TOO
LET'S STOP THESE THINGS FROM STAGING
AN UNDEAD COUP.
LET'S WORK TOGETHER.
TONIGHT!

**TOM.**

WE'LL NEED WEAPONS
THOSE THINGS ARE LOOKIN' MEAN

**HELEN.**

THERE'S SOME RAGS, EMPTY JARS AND KEROSENE.

**BEN.**

WE'LL MAKE MOLOTOV COCKTAILS
THOSE BEASTS WILL PAY.

**HARRY.**

> I'LL THROW THEM OUT THE WINDOW
> I'VE GOT AN ARM LIKE WILLIE MAYS!

**ALL.**

> FORGET OTHER PLANS
> TO HELL WITH THAT TRUCK.
> WE'D JUST SET IT ON FIRE
> AND MAKE IT BLOW UP.
> IF WE GIVE IT OUR BEST
> AND WE DO WHAT WE SAID
> WE WILL SURVIVE
> THIS NIGHT OF THE LIVING DEAD!
> LET'S WORK TOGETHER
> TONIGHT!

> > (**HARRY** *reveals a box of Molotov cocktails and runs upstairs.* **BEN** *cocks his rifle,* **TOM** *swings his baseball bat, and* **HELEN** *uncomfortably wields an axe.* **BARBRA** *does Kung Fu hands.*)

**BEN.** Do it, now!

> > (**BEN** *opens the front door. Bright lights flash through the doorway.* **ZOMBIES** *squeal as they are charred to a crisp. Smoke starts to spill into the room.*)

> > (**HARRY** *races down the stairs. He grabs his tire iron and joins the group.*)

> Great toss. That wiped out a bunch of them. Now let's stay close.

**HARRY.** We're right behind you, Ben. But first, Helen and I have a daughter to take care of.

**HELEN.** Right. We'll meet you out there.

> > (**HELEN** *and* **HARRY** *head into the cellar.*)

**BEN.** Okay. Ready?

**ALL.** Ready!

> > (**TOM** *rushes into the smoke and haze coming from outside.* **BARBRA** *doesn't move.*)

**BEN.** Barbra! Let's go!

**BARBRA.** No! I can't do it!

**BEN.** Barbra look at me! When the time comes, you'll know what to do!

(**GRAVEYARD ZOMBIE 1** *appears in the window.*)

**GRAVEYARD ZOMBIE 1.** GRRRRR!!

(**BARBRA** *screams and punches* **GRAVEYARD ZOMBIE 1** *through the window boards. She looks at* **BEN**, *snatches the rifle from his hands, and moves to the front door.*)

**BARBRA.** Let's go!

(**BARBRA** *exits.*)

**BEN.** Barbra! Wait...

(**BEN** *follows. Lights out on the house.*)

## Scene Sixteen

*(The lights from the flames flicker downstage. A spotlight opens, revealing **BEN**.)*

**BEN.** Barbra? Barbra! I can't see you! Where are you?

*(**ZOMBIE** growls are heard in different areas of the audience. **GRAVEYARD ZOMBIE 1** enters and attacks **BEN**. **BEN** dispatches him easily.)*

Barbra?!

*(**UNDEAD JOHNNY** pops up and grabs **BEN**. As they struggle, **BARBRA** enters.)*

**BARBRA.** Johnny! Stop it! No!

*(**BARBRA** points the rifle at them.)*

**BEN.** Barbra! He's not your brother anymore! Please! Don't shoot!

**BARBRA.** I'm so sorry!

**BEN.** NOOO!

*(**BARBRA** shoots **ZOMBIE JOHNNY** off of **BEN**.)*

Thank you.

*(**ZOMBIE** growls are heard around them.)*

I'll take the gun.

*(**BARBRA** cocks the rifle.)*

**BARBRA.** No. I think I'll keep it. Let's go!

*(Cross-fade to **HARRY** and **HELEN**, grasping a **KAREN** dummy from either side. They pull at her arms as the **KAREN** dummy growls and tries to bite them.)*

**HARRY.** Karen, your mother and I love you!

**HELEN.** But we think this is for the best.

**HARRY & HELEN.** Goodbye!

*(**HARRY** and **HELEN** pull with all their might. The **KAREN** dummy rips in half, her guts spilling onto the floor.)*

*(**HARRY** and **HELEN** toss their halves of Karen aside and embrace.)*

I love you!

*(More **ZOMBIE** groans. Lights out.)*

*(Cross-fade.)*

*(Lights up, revealing **BARBRA**. She's blasting her rifle at the video screen. The screen displays images of different zombies from the film [possibly other films, as well] getting shot.)*

**BARBRA.** Die!

*(Cross-fade to reveal **HARRY** and **BEN** beating on **SHEMP ZOMBIE** in the style of The Three Stooges. They exchange blows until the **SHEMP ZOMBIE** falls to the ground.)*

**HARRY.** Nice work, Ben!

**BEN.** You too, Coop!

*(They shake hands. **BARBRA** enters.)*

You okay?

*(The **SHEMP ZOMBIE** attacks **BEN** from the ground. **BARBRA** blasts him.)*

**BARBRA.** I'm good! Where's Tom and Helen?

*(**HELEN** enters, screaming, as she struggles with a **ZOMBIE** torso that's wrapped around her neck, trying to eat her.)*

**HARRY.** Kill it Barbra!

**BARBRA.** I can't get a clear shot!!

*(**TOM** enters with a baseball bat.)*

**TOM.** Over here!

*(**TOM** slams the head of the **ZOMBIE** torso into the audience.)*

**BARBRA.** Great swing, Tom!

**BEN.** Home run, kid!

**HARRY.** Nice work, Tom!

**HELEN.** Help me up, Tom.

>    (**TOM** *helps* **HELEN** *up.*)

**TOM.** Hey, where's Judy?

**HELEN.** She's fine!

**TOM.** But I want to see her...

**HELEN.** Just... She's fine!

>    *(They hold their ground, waiting for the next Zombie attack. Suddenly the sun rises. It's morning. The* **ZOMBIES** *are all dead.)*

**BEN.** It's over. We did it!

**HELEN.** It's beautiful.

## [MUSIC CUE: "WORK TOGETHER 2"]

**BARBRA & HELEN.**

>    WE WORKED TOGETHER
>    NOW WE'RE UNDEAD FREE.
>    A BRAVE NEW WORLD STANDS BEFORE HUMANITY.

**HARRY.**

>    YA KNOW WE WORKED
>    YA KNOW WE WORKED GIRL.
>    NOW WE'RE UNDEAD FREE
>    BRAVE NEW WORLD
>    HUMANITY, GIRL!

**BEN & TOM.**

>    HERE WE STAND
>    THE VICTORS OF THE FIGHT
>    WE MADE IT TO MORNING
>    WITHOUT A SINGLE BITE
>    OUR UP-ENDED WORLD HAS BEEN PUT BACK UPRIGHT

**ALL.**

>    WE WORKED TOGETHER TO...

>    *(Bang Bang Bang! The group is mowed down in gunfire. They are all dead. Lights down.)*

**[MUSIC CUE NO. 51]**

*(Black & White Picture Montage: Images of the* **CHIEF** *and* **VINCE** *with hooks, dragging the group's dead bodies outside.)*

**JUDY.** *(Offstage.)* Tom! NO!

*(A gunshot is heard and a body hits the ground.)*

**End of Play.**

**[MUSIC CUE: BOWS]**